WANT
ME

CYNTHIA
EDEN

Cover art and design by: Pickyme/Patricia Schmitt

Proof-reading by: Diana Cox of Novel Proofreading

PROLOGUE

Sophie Sarantos woke instantly, knowing that she wasn't alone. Some sound had reached her—a rustle, a creak—*something* that had pushed through the fog of sleep and brought her to consciousness. She didn't waste time screaming. Instead, she reached for her nightstand, desperate to grab the weapon she kept hidden there.

But her fingers never touched the nightstand drawer. Because *he* caught her hand. Trapped her hand in a hard grip. Powerful. Too strong. His fingers were encased in a leather glove and that one glove held her right hand trapped while his other hand—also covered in that leather—closed over her mouth.

"Don't scream, Sophie, you know I'd never hurt you."

No, no, she didn't know that. She knew she was in a dark room with a strange man. A man who'd broken into her home in the middle of the night.

But she didn't fight. She lay still as her mind flashed through a dozen different escape scenarios. She'd had plenty of self-defense classes.

I have to get away from him.

"I was worried about you," he said. He was leaning over her. A big, hulking shadow in the darkness. "I heard what that bastard did to you." His voice was a low, gruff rasp. *Disguised?* "I had to make sure you were safe."

This wasn't happening. She wanted it to be a bad dream, as she'd wanted so many other terrible moments from her past to just be nightmares, too. But they weren't. Her reality was dark and ugly and twisted.

"I'm going to kill him," he swore in that low, rasping voice.

Sophie shook her head. She couldn't speak, not with that glove over her mouth.

"I'll kill anyone who hurts you. Anyone who gets too close. You belong to me, Sophie. Always."

The hell she did. And Sophie lunged up. Her head slammed into his. She wanted to break the bastard's nose. Wanted him *off* her.

He staggered back. Sophie seized that opportunity for freedom. She lunged off her bed and ran for the door.

"*Sophie!*" Her name was a roar of fury.

She yanked open her bedroom door, but he caught her before she could go down the stairs.

His painful grip hurt and she felt the press of a blade against her side.

"You shouldn't run from me," he muttered, his breath hot on her neck. "Never me. Not after all I've done for you."

Screw that. She drove her elbow back against him, as hard as she could. He grunted and his hold loosened for one precious moment. She took that moment and flew toward her staircase.

But he grabbed for her again and she had to twist at the last moment. She stumbled and down, down she went, tumbling and bouncing over those stairs. It *hurt*, but she didn't care, because when Sophie crashed at the bottom of the stairs, she managed to actually get to her feet and run for the door. Her whole body ached, but she was moving and then she was *outside*. The cold, crisp DC air hit her.

His footsteps thundered behind her. Sophie didn't look back. "Help me!" she screamed as she ran forward. She could see the lights from a car approaching on the street. Sophie ran toward those lights, waving her hands. "*Help me!*"

The car stopped with a loud screech of its brakes. A man jumped out of the vehicle. "Miss, miss…are you all right?"

Hell, no, she wasn't all right. She grabbed his coat, clenching it in her fists. "Call the police. *Now.*" She finally glanced back toward her home, the brownstone that had been hers for the last few years. It was dark. Menacing. The front door had been shut. *He* shut it. He'd closed it after she ran outside. *Because I know I left it open.*

He'd shut the door, and he was…waiting for her inside.

***

"We've searched thoroughly," Detective Faith Chestang said as she sighed and faced Sophie, "but we can't find any sign of an intruder."

Sophie stood on her porch. She hadn't wanted to go back into the house, not until the cops were done. *Not until they brought that guy out in cuffs.* Only the police hadn't brought out any perp. And now Faith, a woman Sophie respected, was standing there saying they'd found no sign of him, and…*she's looking at me as if I might be crazy.*

Sophie's chin jerked up. "He was here."

Faith took a slow step toward her. "I know these last few weeks have been hard on you," Faith murmured, her words only carrying to Sophie and not to the uniformed officers still in the area. "Daniel Duvato attacked you in your own home."

Daniel Duvato. Just the man's name infuriated her. Yes, he'd attacked her all right. Right in Sophie's brownstone. He'd knocked her out, given her a lovely new scar when he shattered a lamp over her head, and he'd left her there.

In a home slowly filling with gas.

"You know how victims are," Faith continued, and Sophie stiffened at her sympathetic tone. "Flashbacks are common. It's—"

"I'm not suffering from some kind of post-traumatic stress," Sophie snapped back. "There was a man here, in my bedroom. I woke up, and he was standing over me. He had on leather gloves. He touched me. He...he had a knife."

"Did you see his face?"

"It was dark. I just had an impression of size. He's big." She remembered the feel of his arms around her. "Strong." *Dangerous.*

"If he wore gloves, you know we won't find any prints."

Sophie's shoulders straightened. Yes, she knew that.

"And there's no sign of any forced entry. With the exception of the front door, all of your windows and doors were locked when the cops arrived."

"He was *here*," Sophie said and even to her own ears, she sounded a bit desperate.

Faith rocked back on her heels. Her badge—clipped to her belt—gleamed dully in the faint light on the porch. "I'll keep a patrol in the area tonight."

Forget that. Sophie would be finding a hotel room for the rest of the night. She turned away from Faith and stared out into the darkness. "He said that he planned to kill Daniel Duvato."

Silence.

Sophie swallowed. "He said that he was worried about me. That he had to make sure I was safe." Her hand dropped to her side. Her pajama top had torn—no, not torn. The knife had sliced it open. She'd been lucky that the blade hadn't sliced into her skin. "But you don't keep someone safe with a knife." *You bring a knife in the middle of the night when you want to hurt someone.*

"I'll make sure Daniel's guards are aware of the threat against him," Faith promised her. "And I'll get my team to do another sweep."

But Sophie already knew that sweep would turn up nothing. Her attacker had been too well prepared.

Gloves. A knife. Just what all had he planned for me?

She looked over her shoulder at the detective.

"When he spoke," Faith said slowly, "did you recognize his voice?"

"He was mostly rasping. Whispering." And she *had* wondered if he was trying to disguise his voice. Sophie shook her head. "No, I didn't recognize it."

"A woman in your position has probably made a lot of enemies over the years."

My position?

"Maybe one of those enemies is closing in." Faith took another step toward her. The porch creaked beneath her. "Getting yourself some protection might not be a bad idea. At least, not until I can figure out what's going on."

Protection. Sophie eased out a slow breath. "And let me guess...you have a recommendation for me, don't you?"

Faith nodded. "I happen to know a few men who might be able to help you out in a situation like this one."

She already knew exactly who those men were, even before Faith said—

"VJS Protection. If Chance, Lex, or Dev are on the case, you'll stay safe."

Her heart raced even faster in her chest. She was familiar with VJS Protection, and with one of those men in particular. *Lex.* "I'm not exactly high on their friend list."

"If you're a paying client, they'll take the job. No matter what you've done in the past."

Ah, but Faith had no idea just what Sophie had done. She didn't know about all of the very twisted and deadly secrets that Sophie carried with her.

And those secrets might just be worth dying for.

Or killing for?

Sophie licked her lips. "I'll call Lex." Even though he made her too nervous, too aware.

She'd call him. She'd use him.

Because she had no intention of being anyone's victim ever again.

CHAPTER ONE

A man wasn't supposed to look at a woman and instantly need her. Instantly want her. Instantly imagine her naked and moaning his name.

A man was supposed to be civilized. He was supposed to keep his control.

He wasn't supposed to salivate.

But when Sophie Sarantos strolled into Lex Jensen's office, his control started to splinter. Maybe it was her high heels. Little black spikes that screamed sex appeal. Maybe it was the perfect expanse of her legs, revealed so well in that pencil skirt she wore. Maybe it was her breasts, nice and firm and pushing against the front of her blouse.

Or maybe it was her face—sheer fucking perfection. Heart-shaped, with sharp, fantastic cheekbones. Her lips were full and currently painted a sleek, wet red. And her eyes—no other woman in the world had eyes like she did. A shade of blue that he'd once thought shouldn't be legal. Blue eyes that looked at him and seemed to stare straight into his battered soul.

"Thanks for seeing me," Sophie said.

His cock jerked. *The woman's voice is made for sin.* He had started to imagine that voice, late at night. Whispering his name.

Get your shit under control, man! She's a client! Or, at least, a potential one. Lex kept his position behind his desk and motioned to the chair across from him. "Why don't you take a seat?"

"I prefer to stand."

He almost smiled. Of course Sophie would say that. *Of course* she'd start pacing a bit angrily — nervously? — in front of his desk. The first time he'd met her, he'd been aware of the energy bubbling just beneath her surface. He'd heard others talk about Sophie having ice in her veins. He didn't buy that story for even a minute. She was barely contained fire — fire that was building inside and waiting to explode.

She headed toward the window that looked out over the busy DC street. "Protection. Discrete. Assured. That's what you offer here, right?"

He lifted a brow. "We think of it as the save-your-ass-protection type." His gaze slid to her ass. Such a very nice one it was. But he made himself lift his gaze once more. She wasn't there for him to ogle her. She was there because —

"You got someone who needs protection?" His mind slid through the possibilities. Maybe she had a client who'd pissed someone off. Sophie was one of the best defense attorneys in the area. The more high profile the case, the more likely it was that she'd be in the courtroom. He could easily see her clients needing some—

"I'm the one who needs the protection." She turned toward him. "Me. I'd be the client who needs that 'save-your-ass-protection' that you just mentioned."

Anger sliced through him. A hot, savage blade of fury. "You?" He stalked from around his desk even as the muscles in his body hardened. "Why? What the hell is going on?" Sophie wasn't supposed to be in danger. He'd saved her weeks before. Pulled her out of that gas-filled brownstone. Lex had held her limp body in his arms and felt things—hell, things he had no business feeling. Emotions that he absolutely did not want to analyze. They'd been too dark. Too disturbing.

I wanted to kill the bastard who'd hurt her.

"How much is your fee?" Sophie asked.

"What?" He shook his head and kept closing in on her. "Screw the fee. Tell me what's going on."

But she reached into her handbag—a sleek, expensive little number—and drew out a checkbook.

"Sophie…" Lex growled her name.

She had the checkbook in hand and she was scrawling fast. He reached for her.

She slapped a check in his hand. "Ten thousand dollars. Let's call that a retainer fee. You're working for me now."

His eyes narrowed. The woman was getting under his skin. Before she could pull her hand away from his, he curled his fingers around hers, crushing the check between them. "Why don't you start," he managed from between clenched teeth, "by just telling me what the fuck is going on?"

Sophie's brilliant blue gaze searched his. "I think I need some 'save-your-ass- protection' from you," she whispered. "And now that you're working for me, legally, well, I feel safer telling you certain things."

His temples began to throb.

"It would really help," Sophie continued, pausing to bite her lower lip, "if you signed a non-disclosure agreement. Do you think—"

He yanked her up against him. His right hand kept hers trapped while his left wrapped around her waist. Sophie was a delicate woman. Small. Fragile. He kept forgetting that because of the furious energy that filled the air when he was near her. He had to be careful with Sophie. Had to remember that she was breakable.

He never wanted to break her.

"Screw a non-disclosure agreement," he told her bluntly. "At VJS Protection, our loyalty is to the client. One hundred percent. You need protection? Then, sweetheart, I guarantee you'll have it."

She was still biting her lip. He wanted to bite. He wanted to taste. He wanted to make her moan for him.

And, sooner or later, he'd do all of those things.

But now...

"Who is after you, Sophie? Tell me who the bastard is, and I'll take care of him." Because it enraged him to think of anyone hurting her.

"That's the problem," Sophie told him quietly as she stopped nibbling that lip. "I don't know who he is. I need you to find out. I need you to stop him. And I need you to make sure I stay safe until he can't reach me any longer."

Sophie was scared. He hadn't seen the fear before, but now, he could feel it in the slight tremble of her body. Such a faint tremble, but she was flush against him, so there was no missing it. No missing the quiver of her lower lip. The hitch in her breathing.

His rage built higher.

Sophie shouldn't be afraid.

"Let me go," she told him.

Lex caught himself shaking his head. His fingers had tightened on her. But he wasn't supposed to do that. He definitely wasn't supposed to get all possessive and protective with a client.

But I am.

He forced himself to take a deep breath, and when he did, her scent sank into him. Strawberries. Sweet damn strawberries.

The woman was going to drive him utterly insane.

His fingers slipped away from her. He took a step back and shoved her check into his pocket. Then Lex crossed his arms over his chest — the better to stop touching her — and he locked his glare on Sophie. "I can't help you, not unless I know exactly what is going on."

Her gaze slid away from his. "I woke up last night to find a man standing over me."

What. The. Fuck? He took a quick step toward her, but then caught himself.

"He grabbed me. He was…wearing gloves. He put one hand over my mouth." Her hand lifted and touched her lips, as if she were remembering the attack. "My alarms didn't go off. All those stupid, fancy alarms I had installed after Daniel's attack — they were utterly useless. I woke up because…well, I heard him, I guess. I opened my eyes, and he was just there."

Every part of his body burned with rage. "What did he do to you?" Now that he looked at her more closely, he could see that her makeup was a bit heavier than what she'd worn before. Her cheek…was that a bruise there? Yes, shit, it was. High on her cheekbone.

"I fought him off, but he caught me at the top of the stairs." Her hand dropped back to her side. "I fell and tumbled right down those steps. I didn't break anything, so I was lucky. I managed to get out of the brownstone, and I hailed down a car outside."

He uncrossed his hands. Lowered them to his sides. Instantly, his hands clenched into fists. Some sonofabitch had been in her house?

"By the time the cops arrived, there was no sign of him. Hell…" She jerked a hand through her hair, sending the heavy, dark mane sliding over her shoulders. "Detective Chestang couldn't find any indication that the guy had ever been there. At first, she even tried to hint that maybe I'd just imagined him, because of Daniel."

Just the mention of Daniel's name had him seeing red. That guy had hurt too many people before the cops had thrown him behind bars.

Hurt. Killed.

Now it's your turn to suffer, Daniel.

"I didn't imagine my attacker," Sophie continued with grim pride. "He was there, spouting some bull about needing to make certain I was safe. And he said — he said he was going to kill Daniel for what he'd done to me."

Now his brows shot up. "The guy said that to you?"

"He promised me." She pushed back her shoulders. "I don't want that. I don't want anyone killing for me." Her gaze burned as she stared up at him.

"Tell me more about your attacker," Lex ordered softly.

"I never saw his face. I didn't recognize his voice. I didn't recognize his voice. He was whispering, rasping, so I don't think that *was* his real voice."

Lex waited. *If he disguised his voice, then that means he was afraid you would know him. Shit, it means you do know him.*

"He shouldn't have been in my house." Her breath whispered out. "He had a knife."

For an instant, he didn't move at all. Or, at least, he didn't think he had. But Sophie tensed and then she backed up a step, her gaze widening a bit as she stared at him. "Lex?"

He should unclench his fists. He should give her some kind of reassuring smile. But he was too busy choking back his fury. "You didn't mention his knife before."

Again, she took a small step back. "If he wanted to keep me safe, why break in during the middle of the night? Why come armed with a knife?" She wrapped her arms around her stomach. "I know evil, Lex. I know it intimately.

And I know that man, last night…he is very, very dangerous."

Because the guy sounded like an insane asshole. One who was fixated on Sophie. Maybe it was one of her clients. Maybe it was an obsessed ex. No matter *who* the prick was, Lex would be stopping him.

"VJS…" Sophie murmured. "You guys are the ones who cleared Ethan."

Ethan Barclay. The guy with enough dangerous connections of his own to make Lex's gut knot. He didn't like Ethan. Yeah, they'd proved the guy was innocent in the stalking of another client—a client who just so happened to now be engaged to Lex's best friend, Chance Valentine—but they sure as hell hadn't proved that Ethan was *good*. Just that he hadn't been guilty in that particular case.

Unfortunately, during the course of their investigation, Lex had learned another thing about old Ethan. The guy was Sophie's fucking BFF. "Why aren't you turning to him?" The question came out, and yeah, he was man enough to know it was fueled by jealousy. He didn't like the connection that Sophie had with Ethan. Not one bit.

She looked away. "I don't want Ethan knowing about this situation."

A man broke into her house, with a knife, and that was a *situation*?

"I'm hiring you for your discretion."

"And here I thought it was because you wanted me watching your ass."

For just an instant, her full lips twitched a bit. "That too."

He'd never seen her smile. Not *really* smile. The punch in his gut told him that if he did see that, hell, he'd be in serious trouble.

But the faint twitch in her lips had already vanished. "Ethan doesn't know about what happened last night. My colleagues don't know. I want things to stay that way. We keep this confidential. You keep me safe and your associates…" She waved her hand toward the closed door to his office. "They work with you to track this guy. When we have evidence, we'll turn it over to the cops, and I'll get back to my normal life."

"And until that normal life returns?" Lex pushed. "You're going to have me at your side, day and night, and you don't think anyone will get suspicious about that when—"

"My colleagues know we met weeks ago. When you were investigating Ethan." Her head inclined toward him. "And when you saved my life."

He waited.

"Thank you for that, by the way," she said, her cheeks tinging a bit with color.

"You're welcome."

Her gaze slid from him, then slowly returned. "If anyone asks, we'll just say that we've continued seeing each other. That we've become lovers."

Her voice didn't change. Neither did her expression. But Lex changed. The fire inside of him wasn't about fury any longer. It was about pure, unadulterated need. Because he'd been fantasizing far too much about being Sophie's lover in the last few weeks. Dreaming about her. Thinking too often of her.

"Does that plan work for you?" Sophie asked.

Seriously, did it *work?*

She offered her hand to him. "If so, then we can have a deal."

It wasn't a deal, but he knew that was the way Sophie thought, in terms of deals and contracts. But life wasn't always like that. Still, he closed that last bit of distance between them and curled his fingers around hers. Her hand was so soft, so small in his. And when he touched her, a sensual thrill shot through him. Because he was watching her so closely, he saw the slight widening of her eyes. The faint flare of her nostrils.

It was good to know that Sophie responded to him. It would make things so much easier.

"Deal," he whispered as his hold tightened on her.

***

"Sophie Sarantos is our client?" Devlin Shade asked as soon as he entered the conference room. Lex was already inside, along with the third partner in their growing firm, Chance Valentine.

VJS Protection. V for Valentine, J for Jensen, and S for Shade. They hadn't bothered coming up with some clever name for their business. They didn't need a clever name. They offered protection, plain and simple.

They also hunted.

"She is now," Lex agreed quietly. "Some jerk broke into her place last night and scared her."

"Scared *her?*" Dev repeated as his brows rose. He glanced over his shoulder at the closed door. "I've heard stories about that woman. I think sharks are afraid of her."

Lex's jaw locked. "He had a knife." Now he turned his gaze on Chance. Chance had been silent for the last few moments, as was the guy's usual style. Chance was the old strong and silent type, while Lex was the one who usually went running straight into danger. *The unrestrained and wild type.* Yeah, he knew his issues. "And, according to Sophie, the guy made a threat while he was there." Threat or promise, Lex still hadn't decided which yet. "He told her that he'd kill Daniel Duvato."

Chance's emotionless mask cracked. Right. Because if anything could piss off the guy, it would be the mention of Daniel's name. Daniel had hunted and nearly killed Gwen Hawthorne—the woman Chance loved. Daniel was a sick freak and the guy who just happened to be Ethan Barclay's half-brother. Of course, Ethan hadn't known that shit, and he hadn't known that Daniel had spent years working to take out every one of value to Ethan. When Ethan loved…Daniel destroyed. Because he'd thought that Ethan was interested in Gwen, Daniel had stalked her.

But Chance had stopped that SOB. Unfortunately, he hadn't been stopped before Daniel had hurt Chance, Gwen, Sophie, Ethan…

And Dev.

Too many casualties.

Lex's attention shifted to Dev. Like Chance, the guy now looked seriously pissed.

"Daniel Duvato is behind bars," Chance said, his voice rumbling. "No one will be getting to him."

Lex wasn't so sure about that. And there was something in Chance's closed expression…something that told him Chance knew a bit more about Daniel than he was saying. What the hell was up with that? He, Chance, and Dev had been best friends since they were kids—when they'd been tossed into the same group home for a brief period. Their stay there hadn't lasted, but their bond had.

"Maybe Sophie is the one gunning for Daniel," Dev murmured. "She certainly has cause, right? The guy left her to die."

Lex's shoulders snapped back. "By that logic, you've got cause, too." He pointed at Chance. "So does he."

Chance just stared back at him.

"Cool down, man," Dev said quickly to Lex. "I'm just saying..."

"What the hell are you saying?" Lex didn't like the way Dev was talking about Sophie. Not a bit.

"I'm saying Sophie Sarantos is smart. Crazy, scary smart." There was admiration and wariness in Dev's tone. "She defends the worst criminals in the city every day, and she gets them off. Daniel Duvato hurt her. Worse—at least I think she'd view it as worse—the guy went after Ethan Barclay. From all my research on Sophie…"

And Lex knew Dev had done plenty of digging during that last big case.

"He's the only person she cares about. Daniel hurt him, and knowing what I do about her, well, she just might be the type to want some revenge."

Lex swiped his hand over his face. "You've got this all wrong. She wants protection—"

"Or maybe," Dev said, "she wants an alibi."

What? That was the last thing Lex had expected Dev to say. He rounded on the guy.

Dev lifted his hands. "Hey, don't shoot the messenger, okay? You know this shit. Most folks think she got away with murder once, and if Sophie wanted to kill someone, I'm sure she'd set the stage nicely. I can't think of anyone she'd want to kill more than Daniel Duvato."

This was bullshit. "She's our client," Lex snapped. He had to force his back teeth to unclench. "Not some guilty perp."

"Is there any evidence that someone actually broke into her house?" Dev wasn't backing down. "Or is it just a story she's spinning you?"

He lunged toward Dev.

"Stop." Chance's voice was low but sharp.

Lex didn't stop, though. He grabbed Dev's shirt front and shoved the guy back against the nearest wall. "What the hell is your problem? The woman is a client. She's scared. She wants help. She's not some cold-blooded killer!"

"You didn't read through all the data I found on her," Dev's voice was low. "And don't you wonder, just a bit, why she came to you and not to Chance? Or to me?"

"She knows me better—"

"She can read people. That's one of her things. Size up her enemy in an instant."

"I'm not her enemy." He really, really wanted to drive his fist into his friend's face.

Chance was closing in on them. Growling.

"No, but one look into your eyes, and she would have known you wanted her."

He did.

Chance grabbed Lex's shoulders and pulled him away from Dev.

Dev made no move to straighten his shirt. Or to take a swing at Lex. "I just don't want you hurt, man."

"She's not going to hurt me." The very idea was laughable.

"Isn't she? I saw you at the hospital. I saw the way you paced near her room. You're already in too deep. You don't know it." He jerked his thumb toward the door. "She does. She's a user, bro. She doesn't get close to anyone but Barclay, and I'll be damned if I let her get her hooks into you."

He could only shake his head. Dev was wrong. Flat out *wrong*. "She's the victim. Are we going to help her or throw her to the wolves?" Lex already knew exactly what his plans were.

Chance's grip tightened on Lex's shoulder. "We're helping her, you know it."

Damn straight. "Good. Because I already took her retainer." A check that he'd put in his desk. He shrugged away Chance's hand. "I'm heading back to Sophie's place with her now. You guys can get started on recon to find out just who the hell would want to terrorize her this way."

He turned away.

"Something tells me her list of enemies is going to be long," Dev muttered.

Lex stiffened. He looked over his shoulder. "Are we going to have a problem?" They could straighten that shit out right then.

"It depends." Dev cocked his head. "Are you going to fall for Sophie Sarantos? Because if you do, man, there's going to be hell to pay. I've already seen the wreckage that woman leaves behind." His blue eyes glinted. "I just don't want you hurt like that."

Lex laughed, the sound bitter and rough. "I'm not falling for anyone. I'm doing my job. That's all." He might as well put all of his cards on the table. "I want her." Blunt. Basic. "She knows it. Big deal. Maybe we'll fuck." He sure as hell hoped so. "But it doesn't go past that. You don't have to worry about me being blindsided. That shit just won't happen. I don't get emotionally involved with the clients. Never have. Never will."

Sophie was a case. That was all. He'd do what was necessary to get the job done. Period.

Dev searched his gaze for a moment then gave a grim nod. "Sorry. Just because Chance here fell, doesn't mean you will, too."

Chance's sharp growl got worse. "I'm in the damn room."

"You went fucking to pieces when Gwen was in danger," Dev pointed out. Like they all needed that reminder. "I just don't want to see Lex do the same thing."

Lex rolled back his shoulders. "Big difference. Chance loved Gwen. Sophie...she's just the client." He strode toward the door.

"A client and the woman you want to fuck," Dev said.

He ignored the guy and yanked open the door. Sophie turned, glancing at him sharply. She'd been waiting outside—jeez, since when? He'd left her in his office, and he had a fast moment of panic. Had she overheard what they'd said? Dev's bullshit accusations against her?

But, even though she seemed a bit pale, her gaze was steady. "Is the team on board?"

Even if they hadn't been, he would have still taken her case. He nodded and found himself heading toward her. A lock of her heavy, dark hair had fallen over her eye. He brushed it back. "You're safe, Sophie. You don't have to worry."

Her lips lifted then. That faint smile of hers curled her lips, and all of the breath left his lungs in a sharp rush.

You don't have to worry, but maybe I do.

***

Devlin Shade watched as Lex led Sophie from the office. The guy was already in her web, and he didn't even realize it. When would Lex learn? Black widows killed their mates.

And if there was ever a black widow, it was Sophie.

Chance shut the conference room door. "You've got a problem with her."

More than one.

"What do you know that I don't?" Chance demanded.

He clamped his mouth closed. So far, he just had suspicions—and his gut instinct. Every bit of intel he'd discovered on Sophie had told him that she was one dangerous woman. But he knew that he had to tread carefully now. Especially after the way Lex had just looked at her.

"Dev?"

He rubbed his side. The wound had healed, but he'd never forget lying in that stinking alley, bleeding out, and wondering if his friends were alive. Trust didn't come easily for him. Actually, there were only two people in the world that he did trust.

Chance and Lex. He valued their friendship, and he'd do anything to protect them. "Read my files. See what you think." And he'd get to work investigating Sophie's life even more now—finding her enemies and uncovering all of the skeletons that she still had shoved into the depths of her closet.

He just hoped that Lex could handle what he discovered.

CHAPTER TWO

The brownstone didn't look particularly intimidating. Sophie slammed the car door—the door to Lex's very sleek ride—and stared up at her home. Too bad the place didn't feel like home anymore. Last night's attack had spooked her so much that the thought of going back into that place had her stomach in knots.

"Sophie?"

She glanced over at Lex, and, as always, she wasn't quite prepared for her reaction to him.

Sure, she'd encountered plenty of handsome men in her life. Suave, sophisticated guys. Guys who wanted to wine her and dine her and get into her pants. She knew exactly how to handle those guys. But Lex, he was different.

He wants in my pants, too, though. She wasn't naive enough to have missed that. Only fair, though, considering she'd thought about pouncing the guy herself.

She cleared her throat and tried to study him objectively. His face was hard, strong. He had a perfect square jaw. Cut and defined. Actually, that was how she'd characterize him…cut and defined. A powerful build. Wide shoulders. Obvious strength in his body.

His blond hair glinted in the sunlight. Normally, she wasn't attracted to blondes. She liked men who were tall, dark, and a bit dangerous. Lex was golden—hair and tan skin. His blond hair was thick, but short. His green eyes were dark. Deep. And his face really was almost too handsome.

Until he smiled.

And he was smiling right then. "See something you like?"

She did. Because when Lex smiled, something rather unusual happened. The smile didn't soften him. It made him look harder. More dangerous.

My type.

Of course, she already knew that Lex was plenty dangerous. She'd done some digging on him. After a man saved a woman's life, it was only natural to be curious about him. She'd learned that Lex Jensen was ex-military. That he'd been black ops. The guy knew his way around some deadly situations.

Good—for him, and for her.

He stepped closer to her. They were alone on that street corner. She was wearing a thick coat because DC wasn't showing signs of warming yet—the city wouldn't, not for a while. But as she stood there, Sophie could have sworn that she felt heat sliding from Lex's body. Wrapping around her.

Maybe they should just put everything out in the open. She pulled in a deep breath, hoping it would cool the sudden tension, the fever, that she felt. "You know there's…something between us."

He just stared back at her. Did his pupils widen a bit? Maybe so.

"You want me." There, she'd said it. Just tossed those words out there. All loud and proud.

His smile came again. Half of it, anyway, as his lips hitched a bit. The danger flashed on his face then. "You're used to men wanting you, aren't you, Sophie?"

Yes, she was. She was also well versed in using that desire against men. They didn't care about who she was, not beneath the careful surface she presented to them.

She realized he hadn't answered her question. That was fine. Maybe it was her turn for some honesty. She put her hands on his chest. Tipped back her head. Even in her heels, she was woefully small compared to him.

The bigger they are…

"I thought you should know," Sophie said, "that I want you."

He blinked and she saw shock slide across his face.

Satisfaction trickled through her. His hands lifted, to curl around her shoulders, but Sophie pulled back. "Now, let's get this over with. The sooner we're in and out of this place, the better." Her heels snapped over the sidewalk. It hadn't snowed in over a week, so she didn't have to worry about slipping. A plume of cold air appeared before her mouth when she paused to open her door. It took her a few moments to disengage the locks, and she was aware of Lex standing behind her. A strong, silent shadow.

Not like the shadow that loomed over me last night.

Her heartbeat quickened as she pushed open the door. The brownstone's main door actually led inside into a small foyer. Two other doors were in that foyer, one on the left and one on the right. The brownstone could be split in half and have two perfectly equal living areas. When she'd first purchased the place, she'd had plans to rent out one side of the large dwelling. Only her plans had derailed a bit. She lived in one side of the brownstone, and very slowly, she was working to have the second side renovated.

When she headed for her door, Lex hesitated. She saw him glance toward the other living space. "Nothing is in there but a mess," Sophie said.

"Maybe…"

As soon as she unlocked her door, Sophie's alarm immediately started beeping and she punched in her access code. When she turned back around to face Lex, a furrow was between his brows.

"You didn't have your alarm set last night?"

"Actually, I did." She always set it now. Thanks to Daniel. "I set it right before I went to bed, but it didn't go off."

He slid past her and examined the alarm box.

"It should have gone off," Sophie muttered. That had been bothering her. "If any windows or doors were disturbed, the alarm should have started shrieking."

He grunted and looked back at her. "Doesn't that tell you something?"

"That my alarm is shit?"

He shook his head. "Maybe he was already inside when you set the alarm."

Sophie felt her heart stop. "What?" No, that just wasn't possible. For him to have been inside the house. It-it couldn't be—

"It makes sense. If he didn't break in last night, then that means the guy had to already *be* inside your place. Waiting. Watching."

Nausea churned within her. "Are you trying to scare me?" Because, if so, his strategy was totally working.

"I'm telling you what I think." His eyes gleamed at her. "Now are you ready to show me your bedroom?"

She was ready to get out of that place, ASAP. Sophie intended to stay in a nice, wonderfully luxurious hotel while her place was rewired for security. Again. But for the moment, she straightened her shoulders and headed for the stairs. The bottom stair creaked beneath her foot. Before she could take another step, Lex had wrapped his hand around her wrist, stilling her.

He's so warm.

She hadn't realized that she was still cold.

"You didn't hear that squeak last night, did you?"

Had she? Sophie shook her head as she struggled to remember. "I don't know what woke me up." Something had, luckily. "One minute, I was asleep, and the next...he was standing right above me."

He gave a grim nod. "Then it wasn't the stair that you heard. He was already up in your bedroom. Something in there must have tipped you off."

She looked down at his hand, still holding her. As a general rule, Sophie wasn't so much for touching others. But she liked it when Lex touched her.

She rather liked too many things about him.

Because she did, Sophie pulled her hand from his and she headed up the stairs. She was incredibly conscious of him following closely behind her. He made her nervous, and Sophie heard herself start to talk as she quickly said, "I was at the top of the stairs when he caught me. He grabbed for me, but I-I slipped away — I hit the stairs and tumbled down." That crazy tumble had probably saved her ass. "I rolled down the stairs in a blink and managed to rush out of the house."

"You're lucky you didn't break your neck."

Yes, she knew that. "I'm lucky he didn't kill me," she retorted flatly.

Silence. The thick, uncomfortable kind.

She didn't pause at the landing. She could almost see that SOB standing there, lunging for her. Beneath her coat, Sophie was sure that she had goose bumps rising on her body. She hated being afraid. Fear made her remember her past, and Sophie couldn't stand going back to those terrible days.

She opened her bedroom door. Stepped inside. Light filtered through her thin curtains. The room was just as she'd left it that morning. The four-poster bed was fixed. Her books were perfectly arranged on her shelves. No clutter was out on her dresser or her chest and —

"You like being organized, don't you?" Lex murmured.

No, actually, she didn't.

For an instant, the lid she kept closed on her memories vibrated and she heard a familiar roar in her head. *"Sophie, I've told you too many damn times…clean up your mess!"* Her hand lifted, brushing over her cheek, as she remembered the blow that always followed that refrain. She swallowed back the memory. "My father thought it was always important to keep a clean home."

But he was long gone. So why did she keep letting him haunt her? Sophie's hand moved to rub at the back of her neck as she felt the tension thicken there.

"Nice bed," Lex murmured.

Yes, it was. Her gaze cut toward him, but Lex wasn't looking at her. He was carefully walking around her bedroom, moving slowly on the hardwood. There were no creaks beneath his feet. The boards in her room had never creaked.

So that didn't wake me.

He paused in front of her closet. His fingers lifted, curled around the knob, and when he opened the door, the hinges gave a low, long squeak.

For an instant, her heart seemed to freeze. No, no, the intruder *couldn't* have been inside the whole time. That was…worse, somehow, than him breaking in and coming straight to attack her. The idea that he might have been in her home, watching her all along, when she thought she was safe — *no!*

Lex turned on the light in her closet. She found herself creeping toward him. It was a big, walk-in closet. Shelves for her shoes were on the right. All of her clothes were carefully arranged on the left, put in order by garment type. So neat. So perfect.

Why do I still do that? She shouldn't be letting a ghost control her. Rage built within Sophie, twisting with her fear, and she wanted to grab those clothes and toss them onto the floor.

Instead, she held her body perfectly still.

Lex started pushing her clothes to the side, examining the wall behind them.

She cleared her throat. "You don't really think he's still here, do you?" *He'd better not be.*

Lex paused in front of a small door, one that had been concealed by her clothes. The door only rose halfway up the wall.

"That's attic access," she said quickly. "Storage space."

He opened that little door. A yawning darkness waited inside. Lex stared into that darkness, then said, "It would have been easy enough for him to wait in there, then come out when he knew you were asleep."

Her cheeks burned red hot, then turned icy cold. *Inside with me, the whole time?*

Lex crouched and headed into that darkness.

"No!" Sophie grabbed him. "Let's call the cops, let's—"

"This is why you hired me." His voice was low. So confident. Too confident. "If the bastard is still here, I can handle him."

His fingers slid over her cheek in just the briefest of caresses, warming her cold skin. And then he turned away and slipped through that narrow opening.

Hell. She went in right behind him.

***

Sophie had been a busy woman.

He stared at her house. At the car that didn't belong near her curb.

He'd known that she could come back, sooner or later. He just hadn't realized she wouldn't be coming alone. She was in the house now, with that blond guy who'd touched her far too intimately. What were they doing? Who was he?

Sophie, if you're scared, come to me.

She'd misunderstood last night. Her fear had been so strong. Too strong. She hadn't listened to him. He hadn't been there to hurt her. He'd just needed to make sure she was all right.

Sophie made the wrong choices in life. She always had. She lived too dangerously.

She picked the wrong lovers. Men who were twisted, no good.

She trusted the wrong friends. Friends who would leave her if they ever found out her dark secrets.

She needed him, so very much. And she didn't even realize it.

But that was okay. Soon enough, she would. He knew it was time he stepped from the shadows. Her near-death had terrified *him* far too much. Now was his time of action.

Sophie would soon appreciate all he'd done for her. She'd be overwhelmed. She'd forget the lovers — those fools who should never have been with her — and she'd turn to him.

Finally.

He stared at the brownstone.

But…

Who is that blond bastard with my Sophie?

***

A light flashed on in the attic space, and Lex glanced over his shoulder. Sophie had followed him inside, and she'd just pulled the cord to turn on that overhead light. As he watched her, Sophie wrapped her arms around her waist, shivering a bit. It was much colder up in that attic, but there sure was plenty of space.

Plenty of room for the jerk to hide.

It infuriated him to think that the perp had been in Sophie's house all along. Just waiting, biding his time until he waited for the perfect moment to strike.

"I don't see any sign that someone's been up here," Sophie said, her voice sounding a little too sharp.

She was nervous, afraid. She should be. Because if she had a stalker who'd actually been so confident as to go in her house and stay there while she slept…

And then he'd made the move to approach her, with a knife…

Not fucking good. Those kinds of actions spoke of a serious, dangerous obsession. A fixation that would not end well.

He glanced around the space. There were some old boxes up there. They didn't look disturbed. Nothing really seemed out of place there, at least, not on first glance.

"I don't think he's been here," Sophie said, "and it's cold, so let's just—"

"Is that your gown?" Because he'd just seen the small scrap of red silk that lay pooled near another attic door—a second exit. Another small door that only reached up to the middle of the wall. A door that led—where, exactly? To the other side of the brownstone? The side that Sophie had said she was slowly renovating?

Sophie hurried forward. The attic had been floored so he didn't have to worry about her falling through the ceiling. Before he could stop her, she grabbed that red silk.

Not a gown so much, he realized. It was a very, very sexy piece of lingerie. Sheer in places, lacy in others. Designed to look like pure temptation.

"This shouldn't be up here," Sophie said as she balled the lingerie up in her fist. "It *shouldn't.*"

It was. "Maybe the bastard from last night wanted a memento to keep with him." And he'd brought it up there.

Sophie's body had frozen.

Lex stalked toward her. "You're sure that wasn't up here?"

"I bought it last week, okay?" She licked her lips. "The tag is still on it—*look.*"

And she thrust it at him. The soft fabric filled his hands and, sure enough, a tag was still on it.

Two thoughts pushed through his mind.

You left it because you realized it had never touched Sophie's sweet skin.

A furious thought, aimed at the perp who'd tried to terrorize her.

And…

Who the hell had she been planning to wear that lace for?

A jealous thought because he could all too easily imagine Sophie wearing something like that—for him.

He shoved the garment into the pocket of his coat and he got his control back. Sophie needed his help—not his lust or his freaking jealousy right then. "Where does that other door lead?"

Frowning, she looked over at the door. "To the second side of the brownstone. I told you, I'm still renovating it, so it's a work in progress. But I was...I was planning to rent it out before..."

Before she'd been stalked? Or before Daniel Duvato had attacked her? Because now, her safe haven had been invaded twice. Duvato and whoever this joker was...they were destroying what should have been a secure home for Sophie. He hated that.

He tried to be careful as he opened that second door. He wanted to get a team in to search for prints up there. Not the cops, but a team from VJS Protection. Because he was betting the cops hadn't even bothered to look up there when they'd done their sweep.

When the door opened, he found himself in another closet. He strode out and realized he was in a bedroom, a place that was a mirror opposite of Sophie's room.

No furniture there. Freshly painted walls. The smell of new carpet.

"Is this side of the house wired for security?" he asked her.

Silence.

"Sophie?"

She was right behind him. "I should have thought about this." Now anger hummed in her voice. "I hadn't gotten the workers out to the place since before—before Daniel's attack. But they were here plenty before that night. It would have been so easy for one of them to find the attic entrance. To get into my space." She gave a rough, angry shake of her head. "I should have thought of them!"

"So...you're saying this side isn't wired for security?" Just to be clear.

Streaks of red flamed on her cheeks. "Not yet, but it will be by the end of the day. And those men—I thought I could trust them because they were Finn's men."

Finn? Her voice had softened a bit when she said the man's name. He didn't like that softening. "Finn? Does the guy have a last name?"

"Finn Scott. He always vets his people, so I didn't even consider them." Her breath expelled in a hard rush. "I should have known better." It sounded as if she were berating herself.

"Easy," he told her, trying to make his voice gentle. "This shit isn't on you, sweetheart."

Her head whipped up. Right, he'd just called her *sweetheart.*

Lex cleared his throat and said, "It's not your fault some sick SOB broke into your house. You can't do a background check on every single person you meet."

She blinked.

"This shit isn't on you," he told her once more. "It's on the freak who broke in. And I'll find him." He'd get Chance and Dev to interrogate every man who'd been working there. *Maybe I'll do some personal interrogating, too.* Particularly with *Finn.* Once he was sure Sophie was safe for the day, he'd question the guy.

Her hands fisted at her sides. "In my house. All this time…right with me?" Her eyes were flashed with a tangle of emotions. "I guess you can never be safe, no matter how hard you try."

She rushed past him. He could see the painter's tape then, and the drop cloths that were lining the stairs. She hurried down those stairs. The first floor was definitely still in need of repair. The walls looked as if they were preparing to be primed.

Sophie hurried to the door. She unlocked it, then rushed into the main foyer of the building. The foyer that also led to her home on the right side of the building.

"Sophie!"

But she ran outside, glaring to the left, then to the right. The cold wind sent her hair flying around her face.

He caught her shoulders and spun her around. That was when he realized…she wasn't glaring. She wasn't out there because she was furious.

Sophie was…crying?

Oh, the hell, no.

He didn't like her tears. His chest ached and he found himself pulling her into his arms, crushing her against his chest. And with her against him like that, he was reminded again of how small, how delicate she was.

She fell down the stairs. The bastard had a knife. This wasn't some story she was spinning, it was the absolute truth. Dev had it all wrong.

"I'll get him," Lex promised her. Right then, he might have promised anything to stop her tears. Eyes as beautiful as hers shouldn't ever be filled with tears. Not her. Never her.

What is happening to me?

Her head tipped back. She stared up at him. Her lips were parted and—

He just lifted her up. Lex held Sophie easily because her weight was nothing to him. And he kissed her right there. Kissed her with her held so tightly against his chest. Kissed her with the salty taste of her tears on her lips.

The kiss started easy. Gentle. Maybe it was even just a touch of comfort.

Then it changed, fast.

Because in the next instant, he didn't care about comfort. Need burst to life inside of him. Savage and wild and focused wholly on her. His tongue slid over her lips. Into her mouth. And he feasted.

A moan whispered from her throat, inflaming him more. Her breasts pushed at him, her nipples tight peaks. Her hands closed around his shoulders and she held on with a strong grip. She kissed him back, her mouth moving with a fierce desire to match.

Zero to sixty…fucking fast. Not about comfort. He was kissing her like a starving, wild man. *Only about desire.* Lust. White-hot. So hot that he didn't feel the cold any longer. He could only feel her.

He wanted more.

He wanted everything that Sophie had to give.

And he'd be taking it.

Only…

Not here, not now.

He licked her lower lip. Lex lightly bit that plump temptation. Then he let her slide back down to the ground. Let those sexy heels of hers touch the concrete.

Her eyelashes slowly lifted as she stared up at him. Her eyes—they were darker, hot with lust.

Inside of him, the need built ever higher. *I'll be having her.*

There were no more tears on her face. Her lips were redder, swollen now from his mouth. Her cheeks were flushed with color, and she was truly the sexiest thing that he'd ever seen in his life.

He wanted her naked.

He stepped away from her. "I'm not going to apologize for that kiss."

She didn't speak. She did lift her hand and touch her lips.

"I'd be lying," he said, aware that his voice was gravel-rough, "if I told you that I hadn't thought about kissing you before. See, I've been wanting to taste you from the first moment we met." Back at the police station, weeks ago, when he'd been pretty sure she hated him.

And he'd known he wanted her.

"But I won't do it again," he said, making sure to keep his hands at his sides and *not* grab her again. "I won't, unless you ask for my mouth. Because you can just be a client. I can just be your bodyguard." Was that true? He didn't even know, but he was trying—for her—to play by some kind of rules. A gentleman's rules? Hell, he wasn't sure about that. He'd certainly never been accused of being a gentleman.

A rough soldier? Yes.

A dangerous adversary? Hell, yes.

But—

Sophie turned away from him.

Not a good sign.

"I can be your bodyguard." He had to say this to her. "I can be your lover. The choice is yours, but no matter what..." And he waited until she looked back at him. "I swear, you'll be safe. No one will hurt you while I'm near. *No one*." It was a promise he fully intended to keep.

***

Red blinded him...a furious red to match the rage building inside of him.

Sophie was in front of her home. That blond bastard—he'd been kissing her. Nearly devouring her right there. And Sophie had let him. Not just let him, she'd been on fire for the guy. Grabbing him. Rubbing her body against his. Nearly fucking him *right there*.

Why? Why couldn't she learn? The fast fucks that she picked up...those men never cared about her.

They were just there to hurt her. To twist her up even more. To destroy the girl she'd been.

Now Sophie was walking back toward that too flashy car. He was with her. The blond. Holding open her door. Watching her with need plain to see on his face.

This won't do.

Not at all. The blond wasn't going to get in his way. The blond wouldn't keep him from Sophie.

No one would keep him from her. Not ever again.

The blond bastard would have to go because he would not watch while another man tried to destroy his Sophie. Not again.

The blond was fucking in the way.

So he would be eliminated.

CHAPTER THREE

"No, no, absolutely not," Finn Scott said as he put his hands on his hips and glared at both Dev and Lex. "Hell, *no,* I haven't been sneaking into Sophie's house! And neither have my men!"

Lex narrowed his eyes on the guy. Finn was close to Lex's height, but with a build that was a little thicker. The guy's hair was black, his gaze a dark brown, and he wore jeans and a loose sweatshirt as he stood in the middle of his shop.

"Sophie hired me to do a job. I've been doing that job perfectly well. This is the first I've heard of any complaints." Finn's gaze darted between Dev and Lex. "I have my men thoroughly checked out. No one steals, no one—"

"I didn't accuse you of stealing," Lex said, keeping his voice expressionless. He'd wanted to come to this little chat himself, to get a feel for the guy. He knew Dev was doing his tech work and digging into Finn's past, but sometimes, these up-close meetings could reveal so much more.

"Then what are you saying?" Finn blustered. "I don't like accusations—"

"Who does?" Lex murmured. "But I'm going to need the name and address of every man who has worked at Sophie's brownstone."

For an instant, worry flickered in Finn's gaze. "Not stealing...then what? Did something happen to Sophie?"

Ah, and there it was...exactly what Lex had thought he might find. Real emotion had been in Finn's voice when he said Sophie's name. *Just like hers had changed when she mentioned this bozo.* The guy wasn't just some handyman she'd hired.

Finn took an aggressive step toward Lex. "Where is Sophie? I called today, checking on the job's schedule, but she didn't call me back."

"She's in court," Lex said, his voice smooth. Finn obviously had a problem keeping his emotions under wraps, but Lex didn't. Not right then, anyway. "And the *thing* that happened to her, well, someone broke in her house last night."

Finn's eyes widened.

"The jerk had a knife," Lex continued as Dev remained silent at his side, "but Sophie got away from him."

"She's hurt?"

Again, emotion broke through his words.

"You sure seem very concerned about Sophie..." He and Dev shared a quick glance. Dev had been quiet, just observing—that was the way the guy usually worked.

"Of course I'm concerned," Finn blasted at him. "I owe her far more than I could ever repay."

Now Dev rolled his shoulders and nodded. "Because she got that not guilty verdict for you a few years back." Dev had dug up that intel fast. "It looked like you were going to be facing fifteen years for that robbery, but—"

"But I didn't do it," Finn said as a muscle jerked in his jaw. "And Sophie knew it. She cleared me. I don't steal. I never have, and I make absolutely sure no man on my crew does it, either."

Before Lex had dropped Sophie off at court, he'd questioned her about the guy in charge of her repairs. She'd been adamant that Finn Scott couldn't be involved, and now he was starting to see why. The two of them definitely had a personal relationship.

Sophie, why did you hold that back from me?

"I would do anything for Sophie," Finn told them. "Anything."

Lex gave the guy a grim smile. "Glad to hear you say that." Even if the passion in the other man's tone had Lex's back teeth grinding together. "Because you can start that 'anything' by giving us the names of the men on your crew—names and addresses." Just as he'd said before.

But suspicion flashed on Finn's face. "I don't even know who the hell you are. I mean, you bust in here, throwing Sophie's name around, and you're—"

"I'm the man who's looking after Sophie's interests. The man who is keeping her safe."

Finn seemed to measure him. "I don't remember seeing you with Sophie before…"

Lex opened his mouth to respond, but Dev beat him to the punch. "It's not for you to remember. He's been there. He was the man who pulled Sophie out of that death trap that Daniel Duvato left for her, and he's the man who's been with her since then."

Finn's jaw jutted into the air.

"If you'll do anything for her, then give us the names." Lex held Finn's stare. "I'm asking politely this time. If I have to ask again…" And he bared his teeth, the smile definitely the unfriendly variety. He'd been told by more than a few people that he had a fucking cold smile. A real killer. "It won't be so politely."

Finn swallowed. "I'll get the names. *For* Sophie, got it?"

What the hell ever. He just wanted the list.

Finn turned away. Hurried to his desk. Lex followed behind him and when he got a look at the picture on the guy's desk, the framed image of a smiling Sophie, Finn, and Ethan Barclay, his gut clenched.

That picture wasn't new. It looked like Sophie was about eighteen. Smiling. Happy.

And she'd known Finn for that long?

Hell, that woman had to stop keeping secrets. If she wanted his help, she had to tell him *everything.*

Finn reached out and his fingers curled around the photo. "Didn't know about that, did you?" Finn asked, his voice soft, carrying no farther than to Lex. "You might be her new lover, but I've been with her through the blood and tears."

Blood and tears.

Lex could still taste her tears.

Finn's grip tightened on the photo. "And I'll be there, long after you're gone. Sophie never keeps lovers long these days. You're all expendable to her." His lip twisted. "Same type. Jerks who like to threaten. Jerks who think they have so much power." Then he laughed. "But when are you going to see? When it comes to Sophie, you have no power. You have nothing at all."

***

"I can't go to jail."

Sophie turned her head and met the worried stare of her client. Julianna Patrice McNall-Smith's face was carefully made up, but her fear was breaking up that mask. Causing the makeup to appear too thick. Her lips too red. Her eyes too stark.

"I didn't kill my husband," Julianna said as her fingers fluttered nervously. "I don't care what my stepdaughter is saying. I'm innocent. I didn't do this!"

She patted Julianna's hand. "Relax. This is all preliminary stuff. When the actual trial starts, we'll—"

"Prove my innocence?" Julianna pleaded, voice breaking.

"No." Sophie kept her voice quiet. Most folks had already left the courtroom, but a few people—including the prosecuting assistant district attorney—were still here. "I just need to cast doubt that you're the guilty one. Enough doubt to sway just one person on that jury."

Her words didn't seem to be reassuring Julianna.

"Don't worry," Sophie told her. "We'll show the jurors all of your husband's enemies. We'll get them to see just what kind of man he truly was."

A sadistic, controlling bastard. A bastard with too much money and too much power.

But money and power hadn't stopped his death.

"I didn't do it," Julianna whispered. "I-I don't know what happened. I woke up, and blood was everywhere and—"

And the ADA was closing in. Sophie touched Julianna's shoulder. "We'll talk again later."

Julianna blanched.

"Hello, ADA," Sophie said, raising her voice.

Julianna was still walking around in some sort of dazed shock. Sophie had seen it before. The shock that came when your world collapsed. When you were suddenly faced with losing your freedom. When your friends and family turned their backs on you and the whole world seemed to have gone mad.

Been there, done that, too many times.

Julianna hadn't even noticed the ADA sidling closer.

Sophie had.

The ADA, a handsome, brown-haired man with a grin that flashed his dimples, closed in on her. Only he didn't flash his dimples. Sophie knew that Clark Eastbridge saved his dimples for important people—like juries.

"She got your bail, not real surprising, is it?" Clark murmured. "Sophie is the best."

She smiled at him. Okay, she bared her teeth. She and Clark spent far too much time as opponents. She'd heard he was a decent guy, but since he was usually trying to toss her clients into some dank, dark cell someplace, she'd never actually seen the decent side of him.

Guilty until proven innocent. She figured that was his motto.

"You took my client's passport. You insisted on a two-million-dollar bond…" She kept her grim smile in place. "Don't you think that was excessive?"

The faint lines near his eyes — a blue that was darker than Sophie's own — tightened a bit. "I think stabbing a man thirteen times is excessive." His voice — smooth and deep — rolled over her. Clark shrugged. "But that's just me."

Julianna whimpered. No other word for it. A full-on whimper. "I didn't! I-I don't know what happened—"

Oh, hell. Time to stop the client from saying anything else. If they were going for an insanity defense, Sophie would deal with that whole not-remembering bit later.

"We're done." She patted Julianna on the shoulder. Hard. "My associate, Kurt, will take care of you. You'll be out on bail before you can blink."

Julianna was blinking at her — blinking away tears. "Thank you. You believe me when no one else does."

It actually wasn't her job to believe her clients. It was just her job to defend them. But when Julianna came in for a hug, Sophie embraced the other woman. She even heard herself reassuringly say, "Don't worry. Everything will be all right." That was so crazy. She *never* made vows to her clients like that.

It was just that—in spite of all her money and the power that Julianna had once wielded—she seemed so broken to Sophie.

Sophie glanced over Julianna's shoulder. Sophie's assistant, Kurt Blayne, was already on his feet. He'd been second chair for her that day, and the guy knew his stuff. He was an up-and-coming defense lawyer at her firm, and she knew Kurt would go far. His good looks would work wonders for jurors and his sharp intellect—it would definitely help his client.

"I'm going to take care of you," Kurt told Julianna, using a soft, reassuring voice. "Don't worry. Sophie handles the judges, and I make sure the clients get home safe."

He also had orders to stay close to Julianna—to make sure she didn't talk to the press or any little…visitors…that a sneaky ADA might send her way.

Sophie didn't speak again until Julianna and Kurt were gone. Then she lifted her right eyebrow—a trick she liked to use on difficult witnesses, a look that she knew totally called bullshit—and she said, "You honestly believe that woman took a knife and stabbed her husband again and again? A man who outweighed her by sixty pounds? A man who was nearly a foot taller? A man who—"

"I think I don't buy her innocent act. And I think you're too smart to do it, too."

"I'm smart enough to recognize a victim when I see one." She started gathering her things together, shoving her notebook back into her briefcase, snapping up her tablet, and —

He touched her hand. "She isn't you. None of the people you defend — they aren't you."

Sophie swallowed, hating the burn of shame that filled her. She and Clark hadn't attended the same college and definitely not the same law school. They sure as hell hadn't grown up in the same neighborhood. He was Ivy League, a rich boy from day one. Born to wealth and privilege.

She wasn't.

But Clark *would* have access to all her records. Everyone at the DA's office would. So that meant plenty of people in this town knew about her painful past.

She stiffened her shoulders and lifted her chin. Rumors and whispers had followed her for years. She'd *never* let anyone see that those rumors and whispers cut her like knives. "I never said she was me. If it had been me..." Now she locked her gaze on him. "I would have fought back after the first beating. She didn't. She let him hurt her again and again. And I'll prove in court that he was the aggressor, not my client."

Clark whistled. "Like that, is it? Going for the old battered spouse story?"

"It's not a story." That jerk would know nothing about abuse. "I'm going for my client's freedom. That's all." He was still touching her. She didn't like it. His touch didn't make her warm, not the way Lex's did. In fact, he was nothing at all like Lex.

Or like the men she dated. She needed men with an edge. Men with a darkness that clung to them.

Not men who only saw the world in narrow terms of black and white. Innocent and guilty.

Sometimes, the innocent *could* be guilty.

And the guilty could be innocent.

"Get your hand off me," Sophie said, not even bothering to be polite about it. As if she had a reputation for politeness in justice circles. She knew good and well that most thought she was a hard-ass, and she liked that. Folks in her business didn't respect someone who could be easily pushed around.

So, no, politeness wasn't her concern then. She just didn't want him touching her.

He's not Lex.

That thought shot through her head and made her uncomfortable.

He immediately removed his hand. "I'm sorry, I…" Clark exhaled. "Look, how about we go someplace and talk? I sure didn't mean to piss you off, okay?"

Now she eyed him with suspicion. "Why the nice act?"

His gaze slid away.

"Clark…"

"I *might* have heard about your break-in last night. I just—I wanted to see if you were all right."

There was no *might* in the equation. The ADA had been sharing gossip again. If her spine got any straighter, Sophie feared it would snap. "Did your cop buddies try to tell you that I imagined the whole thing? Because I didn't."

He reached out toward her, then stopped, his hand clenching into a fist. "Of course you didn't. I *know* you. You aren't a woman given to fantasy—"

Actually, on that, he was wrong. She fantasized plenty. *Mostly about Lex.*

"If there's something I can do to help you, I will. I'll send more cops to patrol your neighborhood tonight. I can make sure you're safe while you're there and—"

A strong, male voice said, "She won't be there tonight, Eastbridge, but thanks."

The voice was commanding, vibrating with power, and very close. A tingle of awareness shot through Sophie at the deep rumble and she looked back to see Lex closing in on her.

Was just the sight of a man supposed to make her heart race? Supposed to make her sex clench? Because that happened. Just the sight of him…and that dangerous smile of his.

A smile that held no dimples.

Only deadly promise.

"Sophie will be with me tonight, Eastbridge," Lex continued. He was now close enough for her to inhale his rich, masculine scent. "But still send your cops by. Maybe they can catch the SOB who tried to hurt my lady."

His lady? She lifted her right eyebrow at him. *Bullshit.*

But then he leaned toward her. His fingers brushed her cheek, just the back of his knuckles in a careless kind of touch.

Heat flooded her. Her nipples tightened.

No! She was in a courtroom, for goodness sake! The ADA was frowning at her and—

Lex kissed her. A hot, deep, I-don't-care-who-is-watching kiss. Totally unprofessional. Totally awesome. Totally *make-me-want-to-strip-him.*

When he pulled back, her breath was coming in pants. So was his. Maybe that kiss had been fake. For show. Maybe he'd kissed her to live up to his part of the bargain because she'd told him that she didn't want others to know she'd hired VJS and—

"I missed you," he told her simply.

He sounded sincere. Her stupid heart raced even faster. When had any guy *ever* said that he missed her? Said it and meant it? She forced her lips to curl a bit. Forced herself to say, "I missed you, too." Only, as soon as she said those words,

Sophie realized they were true. She *had* missed
him. She'd caught herself thinking about him
again and again during her court session. She'd
wanted him near not because he was her hired
protection, but because —

She wanted him.

Clark coughed. "I, um, think you have me at
a disadvantage."

He was at a definite disadvantage when
compared to Lex.

Lex eased back. He kept a grip on Sophie's
wrist, lightly circling her with his fingers.

"You know me," Clark continued. "But I
have no idea who you are."

Lex just laughed, but the sound was cold. "Of
course, you do. Your boss hired me to run some
protection work a few months back. When he
started getting those death threats, and he didn't
think in-house security would cut it."

She saw Clark widen his eyes. "VJS
Protection. You—" He looked back at Sophie.
"You hired him to protect you?"

Lex brought Sophie's fingers to his lips.
"Does it look like she hired me, Ace? You should
be faster on the uptake, being an ADA and all."

She felt the edge of his tongue slide over her
knuckles. Her breath whooshed out.

She was pretty sure he was making her wet.
She'd obviously gone way too long since having
a lover. Her body was in an overdrive reaction.

"Sophie and I have been involved for a while," Lex continued smoothly. "The fact that some jerk tried to scare her last night? That shit pissed me off. A lot. So until I catch him, Sophie will be staying with me."

Wait, he sounded as if he meant that last part. Staying with him had *not* been part of the deal. She had her swank hotel room already booked. She'd thought about splurging for an in-room massage because the day truly had been a bitch.

There had been *no* plans to spend the night with Lex, tempting though the idea was.

"Then I guess Sophie and I won't be having that drink tonight," Clark muttered as he jerked at his tie.

"Not tonight," Lex agreed easily. "Not any night that I'm around." His dangerous smile was still in place. "I think you missed your window, Ace. She's taken."

"*She's* right here," Sophie said, pushed too far. Right. It had been her idea for Lex to pretend to be her lover. But no one had said the guy needed to go all caveman. Especially in front of the ADA! Jeez, something new for her to live down. Awesome. "And she's ready to go." She nodded briskly to Clark. "I appreciate your offer of the extra patrol cars, and I'd love for them to go around the brownstone. I also think..." She had to say it. "I also think that Daniel Duvato needs extra security. The man at my house

threatened him. He said he was going to kill
Daniel for what he'd done to me."

A furrow appeared between Clark's perfect
brows. "And you believe him? I mean, he could
have just been some nut job—"

"He could have," she agreed. "But—"

"Duvato is already in maximum security. No
one will be getting to him." He hesitated. "But I'll
go by tomorrow, okay? I'll personally check
things out for you."

Her breath expelled in a quick rush. "Thank
you."

Clark shook his head. "The guy tried to kill
you, and now you're working to save his hide?
Careful there, Sophie, or your icy reputation will
start to crack. People will see you for the woman
you really are."

No one ever saw her for the woman she
really was—that was a good thing.

Clark took his bag and left, but she stood
there a moment longer. A guard was near the
door, but, otherwise, it was just her and Lex in
the courtroom. The guard was too far away to
overhear her. "What the hell…" Sophie
demanded in a lethal whisper. "Was that about?"

He shrugged. "The guy wants you."

"He's the ADA! Half the time, I think he
hates me, he—"

"I know the signs. I saw the way he was
looking at you."

Insane. "What way?"

"Like he wanted you naked."

She rolled her eyes. Grabbed her briefcase. And marched past him. *Men.* She needed to be saved from men and their idiocy. When she passed the guard, Quincy gave her a slow nod. She inclined her head toward him. "Night, Quincy." She liked him. The guy was a serious fixture at the courthouse — and whenever she could, she snuck him some gourmet chocolates.

And in return, he paid her back with gossip.

She kept up her fast march toward the elevator. She jabbed the button, every muscle in her body feeling taut as she waited and waited and —

The doors opened. She shot inside. Lex followed — more slowly — behind her. As soon as those doors closed —

"You don't have to worry about the ADA wanting me. You don't have to worry about any man wanting me," she snapped at him. "I'm a grown woman. I am perfectly capable of — "

"Your stalker wants you. He's clearly obsessed. He took your negligee, for shit's sake." Real anger quaked in his words. "You're a sexy woman. Beautiful. A fucking walking dream."

Wait, she was? Since when? Usually, she just felt like a nightmare.

"It was your idea for me to pretend I was your lover, remember?" He glared at her. "I could have just told Eastbridge the truth."

She stood toe to toe with him. Her head tipped back as she glared just as hard—and tried not to feel the desire that kept pulsing through her. Anger was *not* supposed to be some kind of aphrodisiac, not even in her twisted world. "It wasn't my idea to say I was staying with you tonight. That I was practically living with you!"

His eyes narrowed. "A psycho with a knife broke into your place last night."

Like she needed that reminder.

"And you thought you'd just sleep there alone?"

"I got new security installed today." Security that wasn't completely done, unfortunately. "But no, I'd planned to stay in a hotel tonight."

He swore. "Wonderful. A place with total access for the general public. Super secure."

He was making her insane. "I was going to stay on a secure level." *Because I'm not an idiot.*

He locked his fingers around her upper arms. She almost forgot to breathe. That electric connection she felt when he touched her was just *so* not normal. Her whole body was overheating now. And she was actually inching closer to him. Wrong, wrong. *Wrong.*

But he sure felt right.

The bad boys always did.

"You'll be plenty secure with me."

Her breath came a little faster. And his right hand rose to curl under her chin. She almost flinched away from him because his touch seared her too much.

"Are you afraid of me?" Lex asked her.

"No." She was a very good liar.

"Then why are you scared to stay with me?"

The elevator doors opened. A quick glance showed Sophie that they were on the main street level. He'd dropped her off at the courthouse earlier, and she'd just assumed he'd found a garage nearby to park his car.

He didn't move to leave that elevator. "Sophie?"

"I'm not afraid of you. Okay?" Ready to leave, she stepped to the right.

So did he. The guy was blocking her escape path. Annoying. She looked up at him and saw that determined glint in his eyes.

Sexy. Damn it.

Fine. If he wanted some sort of confession, she'd give him one. "I'm afraid of what might happen between us."

He finally got out of her way. Good. She marched through the lobby and headed for the street.

He grabbed her briefcase.

"What are you —"

Lex held up his hand. "Easy. I'm just being a gentleman. Carrying your briefcase. That's all."

"I don't trust gentlemen." Her words were out before she could pull them back. But, hell, since she'd already said them… "I prefer men who face danger without flinching. Men who don't mind getting dirty." In more ways than one.

She strode forward. The sun had started to sink and the evening air definitely held bite. "Where are you parked?" Sophie asked him. They'd get to his car and get out of there.

Would they go back to his place?

Um, *no*.

She'd have him drop her at the hotel. Because if they went back to his place, Sophie was afraid her control wouldn't hold. She had one serious weakness.

Dangerous men. Fierce lovers. He was both.

No, it was better not to spend the night with him. Better to just get the guy to leave her at the sanctuary of the ritzy room she'd reserved and just not walk down that particular dark road.

She knew how destructive desire could be.

"This way." His fingers took hers. Laced with her hand as if they were lovers just taking a stroll down the road. To onlookers, that was probably exactly what they appeared to be.

She didn't pull away from him, though she did think about it. His soft laughter told her he knew, and he held her hand even tighter.

They stopped at the street corner. It was just the two of them, no one else close by while they waited for the light to change. She could see his car now, on the other side of that road. He'd lucked out and gotten a prime spot.

"I think you have the wrong idea," Lex said, his voice low and intimately close. He'd bent his head, and his breath brushed lightly over her cheek.

She wondered if he was about to kiss her again.

She wanted him to.

"What idea is that?" Sophie asked him, aware that her own voice had gone husky. Sensual.

"You think I'm a gentleman. But, sweetheart, nothing could be further from the truth." His gaze was on her mouth. "And I sure do excel at dirty."

I don't think you're a gentleman. I know the truth about you. It was way too hard to breathe. His mouth was so close. She wanted his lips on hers and—

"The light's changed."

What? Oh, crap. Damn him. Now he was looking all confident and cocky. She jerked away from him and started marching across the street. His laughter followed behind her, and she glanced over her shoulder, glaring, and saw that he was trailing a few steps behind her. "Funny, Lex, very—"

The roar of a car's engine cut off her words. Her head jerked to the right and she saw a big, black SUV barreling toward them. Coming far too fast.

She screamed, an instinct, but in the next moment, Lex's rock-hard arms were wrapping around her. He lunged forward, holding her tightly against him, and they seemed to fly through the air as that vehicle raced right past them, close enough that she could smell the rubber from the tires and feel the heat of its engine.

Then she and Lex were tumbling onto the cement. He took the brunt of the fall, cushioning her. Sophie's breath choked out as she struggled to shove her fear back down.

Someone nearly ran us down! Right here! In front of the courthouse!

"You're not hurt." Lex's voice. His hands ran frantically over her back, her arms, her legs.

"No." She shook her head. "I'm not hurt." But she could have been. They both could have been. She looked toward the street. When Lex had grabbed her, he must have dropped her briefcase. Notes and papers littered the road where they'd been just moments before.

Moments.

She looked back down at Lex and realized that she was straddling him. When had she gotten into that particular position? Voices rose around them as others realized what had happened and rushed toward them. "You saved my life," she said.

He smiled that dangerous grin and he sat up, but kept a hold on her so she couldn't slip away from him. "Guess what?"

Was he serious?

His fingers curled under her chin. "There is no fucking way you're staying alone in a hotel tonight."

Then he kissed her. Hard. Frantic. Angry.

"Because he *won't* hurt you," he growled against her lips. "He won't."

CHAPTER FOUR

She hadn't argued again about the hotel. Lex figured a little hit-and-run could sure change a woman's mind. But Sophie had insisted on stopping by her place so she could pack a bag. Lex had stayed by her side while she packed, not about to let any other danger come her way, then he'd raced them to his place.

A few moments before, Lex had lit a fire in his den. The flames crackled and danced, and Sophie stood just a few feet away, her gaze seemingly fixed on the fire.

He didn't have a place directly in DC. His home was just outside of the city, situated for premium privacy. He didn't like nosey neighbors. Didn't like others in his space. They were secluded at his place. Secluded and…
"You're safe."

She jumped, and he wondered if she'd actually forgotten that he was there. But then Sophie shook her head. "Safety's an illusion. We tell ourselves that we're safe every day, but we're not. Danger is always out there."

Danger had come far too close that evening. Close enough that the cement had torn through his clothes and scratched up his arms. When he'd heard that growling engine, he'd jumped toward her. Nearly fucking flown in his haste to reach Sophie.

In that one moment, he'd been afraid. Terrified that he wouldn't get to Sophie in time.

As a rule, he didn't normally fear. But because of Sophie, he'd felt the acid of fear eating at him twice within the last few months. That evening and also weeks before, when he'd found her crumpled body inside her brownstone.

"It's a good thing ADA Eastbridge showed up on the scene," she said, rubbing her arms.

Bullshit. There was nothing good about that guy.

"He'll check the traffic cams for us. Hopefully, we'll get a hit on the driver."

Not if the driver hadn't wanted them to track him. It was all too easy to steal a car and use that vehicle for your crime of choice. DC was filled with people. Too many people equaled plenty of opportunities for evil.

"I like your place," Sophie said as her gaze stayed on the fire.

His brows shot up. She liked this? "It's stark." He should probably put some pictures on the walls. Maybe hang up a painting. Put down one of those expensive-ass rugs. Decorating had never been big on his to-do list. Her place, though, it had been fancy. Like something out of a magazine.

"You're stark, so it fits."

Was that an insult? He wasn't sure.

"Warm and solid. Strong." She glanced around her. "Wood furnishings, leather. A giant TV. Looks like a man's paradise."

With her there, it was.

"I should go to bed," Sophie said as she shook her head. "It's not like I slept much last night." She turned and faced him.

"You'll be safe here."

"I know."

He pointed to the hallway on the right. "Take the first room." His room. The only one with a bed because he didn't exactly have a lot of guests. He'd bunk down on the couch and try not to imagine her stretched out in his bed.

She started to walk by him. He hated to say it, but… "You didn't tell me that you and Finn Scott were lovers."

She kept walking. Headed for the hallway. "I don't remember you asking."

He locked his knees so he wouldn't follow her. "I need to know all of your lovers, Sophie. If someone is obsessed with you, obsessed to the point of breaking into your home and coming at you with a knife, then it could be—"

"A man I fucked?" Now she did look back at him. But the only light in the room came from the fire, so shadows hid her expression from him. "It's not like I had any deep, lasting relationships with my lovers. I don't have deep relationships."

"Finn seemed quite dedicated to you."

"Because he was a lover once, but a friend much longer."

Once?

"I didn't tell you that I'd slept with him because I wanted you to be able to make your own judgment about him." She seemed to hesitate. "Do you think Finn would do something like this to me?"

"I think the guy has a whole lot of anger issues, and I think he might not have clued in on the fact that he isn't lover material for you any longer." That damn photo had gotten on Lex's nerves.

She laughed. "Oh, you'd be surprised. Finn knows me well."

What was that supposed to mean?

She turned away, obviously done with her little share time. But Lex wasn't done, not even close. So much for standing firm and not following her. He headed after her, and caught Sophie just before she entered his bedroom. "If you want my help, then you need to tell me *everything* about yourself. I need to know the names of your lovers. I need to know who they are so I can investigate them and make sure one of those bastards isn't running around with a knife—or driving a black SUV and trying to mow us both down!"

She was silent.

He hated it when she got silent. "Sophie…"

"What do you think?" Sophie asked as she tilted her head. A lamp was on in his bedroom, so he could see the delicate lines of her profile. "That I have this amazingly long list of lovers that I'm going to share with you?"

"You said you had preferences when it came to your lovers." Those words had burned into his mind. "You want a man who isn't afraid of danger. A man who doesn't mind getting dirty." He'd love to show her how dirty he could be.

"I do enjoy men with a certain edge, but I don't always indulge that particular need." Her voice was soft, a seduction in itself. "I know it's risky to let someone get close."

He was close to her right then.

"Do you really need that list?" Sophie continued, seeming to hesitate. "To do your job?"

Yes. "You can tell me or Dev will just dig into your past and find it out for me." He shrugged. "Having you tell me on your own just seemed easier."

"Dev," she repeated the name, her voice slightly wooden. "He's the one so good with computers, right? A few taps on the keyboard, and he finds all your little secrets."

He wasn't surprised that she knew about Dev's skill set. A woman like Sophie would have done her research on VJS Protection.

"Has he already found some of my secrets?" Sophie asked as she stepped closer to Lex. Her tone was different. Angry. Desperate? She put her hand on his chest, as she gazed up at him. She still had on her heels. He didn't even know how in the hell she hadn't lost those things during the commotion on the street.

"He found some," Lex allowed. Why lie?

"What did he learn?"

His hand rose and slid down her arm. He'd been playing nicely with her so far, but if the woman was determined to hold back on him, she was just putting herself in greater danger. He couldn't allow that. To unmask her stalker, he needed to know everything about her. And, yeah, he had Dev hacking into her past. Dev *was* looking for her lovers. But Lex wanted Sophie to trust him enough to actually *tell* him about her past.

"What did he learn?" Sophie said again, her voice sharper.

His fingers slid over her. First her arm, then his hand curled around her hip. "When you were a girl, you spent a lot of time in the hospital, didn't you?"

He heard her sharply indrawn breath, and he almost stopped.

Almost.

But her life was on the line. The bastard out there wasn't just playing some game. He was a threat that had to be eliminated.

And I already told her that I'm no gentleman.

His hand slid up her ribcage. "Broken arms, broken ribs. So many accidents for such a young girl."

She trembled beneath his touch.

"The police were called in a few times, weren't they?" Lex asked her.

"The ER docs have to report," Sophie whispered.

He leaned toward her. "Did those doctors think you were being abused, Sophie?"

Silence.

"They did, didn't they? You were hurt so much." And it pissed him off. "But the cops didn't stop the pain, did they?"

"No one stopped it." Her voice had gone flat. Completely cold.

"Who hurt you?" Lex asked. "Your mother? Your father? Both of them?"

"Stop it."

"Someone was hurting you. For years. Dev got access to your medical reports, so we know what went down. The cops didn't stop the abuse. You just kept being hurt." Not just hurt, tortured.

"Where was your good buddy Ethan back then? Why didn't he help you?" Because he knew they'd grown up together. Sophie and Ethan Barclay. "Or good old Finn. I saw the photo of the three of you."

She shook her head.

"You, Ethan, and Finn. You all looked barely eighteen. If both of those guys were there back then, why didn't they help you? Why didn't they—"

"Stop it!"

Exactly. "Why didn't they stop it, Sophie?"

She shoved against his chest. "Don't talk about Ethan, understand?"

Ah, and they were back to that. Her almost fanatical loyalty to the guy. "You're so close to him, but Ethan isn't here, is he? Why didn't you go to him for protection?"

"I don't want Ethan to know—"

"*Why the fuck not?*" His fury exploded.

"Because Ethan would kill for me!" The words came out of her as a scream and he knew her control had broken.

Sophie clapped her hand over her mouth.

But the damage had already been done.

"Did he kill for you before?" Now things made sense. "Your parents…their murders were never solved, were they? The cops had suspicions that you were involved, but they never pressed charges against you. Hell, how could they? You had medical reports a mile long. No jury in the world would have ever convicted you."

But Ethan Barclay would have been another story. Had she covered for that man, all those years? Because, judging by the passion in her voice, she absolutely believed Ethan would kill for her.

She pulled her hands from him. Straightened her shoulders. "You don't know me."

"Because you won't let me know you." Suddenly, what she'd said before made sense. "Once," he said, throwing that one word back at her. "You said that you and Finn had been lovers once. You meant that. You only slept with him once." More details started to click for him and he spoke faster, saying, "You told me...you just said that you didn't let people get close, but lovers are close, aren't they, Sophie?"

She backed up a step. "I'm done for the night. I'll answer your questions in the morning."

In the morning, her control would be back in place. In the morning, she'd have nice, pat, *safe* answers to give him. He didn't want safe. He wanted real. And if he had to keep pushing her, so be it. Just more sins to add to his already blackened soul.

But she'll be safe. I'll know her secrets so I can protect her.

"You take dangerous lovers." This was all info she'd revealed to him, but now he'd put the pieces together. "Because they're men you won't fall for, right? You seduce them, they seduce you—whatever the hell your game of choice is. But it's just *once,* right? You don't stay with your lovers long. Just—"

"Once," Sophie said flatly. Her gaze glinted up at him. "That's all I need. I'm not looking for some kind of forever. Some lasting love. I know that's all just BS. But we all need pleasure every now and then, don't we? We need to feel like we're not alone in the dark."

He stared down at her.

"You want a list? Fine." Her voice was too brittle. "You already know about Finn. I was with him when I was eighteen."

He'd pushed, but he didn't want—

"Alec Farrell."

His stomach muscles clenched.

"I think I was twenty-one then."

He fucking knew the guy's name. And he'd heard plenty about the man's ties to organized crime.

"Kurt Allan."

Another name that was familiar. The guy was a music mogul—one who'd crashed and burned hard after his brother was found murdered in Kurt's hotel room.

Shit, had Sophie defended the guy in that case? He thought she might have.

"Bruce Mitchum."

Now he had to fist his hands. He actually knew that guy — personally. Bruce was an ex-SEAL, and they'd crossed paths more than a few times. Bruce had always struck him as a serious jerk — a man who sought out danger and said to hell with the consequences.

Yeah, she definitely seemed to have a type all right.

He waited for more names to come. He was damn well braced for them.

Sophie kept glaring at him. "Happy now?"

No, he was — "Wait, that's it?"

She huffed out a hard breath. "I don't like for people to get close, but sometimes, I just — I need, Lex. Dammit, I need, too."

Then she spun away. Sophie's hand flew out and he knew she was going to slam that door shut on him.

And it was too much. He'd pushed, but he hated the tremble in her voice. Hated the idea of her with any other man —

But me.

His feelings weren't rational. He wasn't rational. Lex didn't care. He grabbed the door before it could slam on him. His fingers curled around the wood and he shoved it back. "You think you're the only one who needs something in the dark? Someone?"

She stumbled back, then stilled.

She didn't tell him to get the hell out.

Her mistake.

"You like danger, Sophie? The thrill that comes with the fast hookups?" Finn didn't fit that bill—not exactly—but had the others truly just been one night stands for her? "I can give you that thrill. Right here. Right now." It was wrong. They were both still riding the edge of adrenaline from that near run-in with the black car. He'd pushed too much. He'd—

Sophie tossed her blouse aside. "Right here." She just stripped the garment off in a flash.

What. The. Fuck?

She had on a black scrap of a bra. Her breasts spilled forward.

"Right now."

She pushed down her skirt. She had on thigh-highs—seriously sexy thigh highs that made his already erect cock surge even more.

"Once is always enough for me. Once, then we get back to life as normal." She stood before him in her underwear, those insanely sexy thigh highs, and those make-me-beg shoes, and she was actually telling him that once would be enough.

No way.

He touched her, aware that his fingers shook a bit when he slid them against the smooth skin of her arm. When a man was offered a waking wet dream, a little shake was normal. "Once…"

His voice was too rough. "Once will be one hell of a start."

He wasn't like the others. He didn't want the quick thrill of touching a woman like her.

He wanted her.

For fucking keeps.

He lifted her up against him and his mouth took hers. There was no restraint. No gentleness. No holding back. He was too far gone for that, and he knew that she was, too.

He feasted on her as they staggered to the bed. His hands roamed over her back, down to the lush curve of her ass. The silk of her underwear was in his way, and he wanted that scrap gone. He wanted her, just her.

He put her on the bed. Right in the middle of that king-sized bed. He'd fantasized about her there so many times.

He'd done this — pushed too much, and now they were both going up in flames. He should stop, he should —

"Stop now, and we'll both be sorry," Sophie said.

Her legs were spread and his gaze couldn't leave the apex of her thighs. He dropped right there. Fell to his knees by the edge of the bed and yanked her toward him. Her legs slid against his shoulders and he put his mouth against her sex. The lace grew wet — from his mouth, from her, and her sharp moan was perfect music to his ears. She arched toward him, slamming her hips up, and his fingers jerked that scrap out of his way so that he could taste her.

She always smelled like strawberries, but she tasted far, *far* sweeter. He licked her. He sucked. He thrust his index finger into Sophie and made her moan again. He loved the wild pant of her breath. Lex was going insane for her taste and—

She came against his mouth. Hell, *yes*.

He surged up. Because he was damn lucky, he managed to yank open his jeans and actually get a condom on in near record time. There were no more preliminaries. There was nothing but her. He drove deep into Sophie, and the contractions of her release immediately had her sex clenching tightly around him.

Tight. Tight. She is so fucking tight.

So good that he nearly exploded right then. His hands fisted on the covers because he was actually afraid of touching her. Afraid he'd be too rough and bruise her because he was that far gone. He leaned over that bed, and he drove into her. Hard. Deep. Again and again, and her legs rose to wrap around him.

He needed to see her breasts. One hand yanked at her bra, and the material seemed to tear away. Her breasts—with pretty pink nipples—thrust up toward him. He took one in his mouth, and Sophie's sex clenched around him again. Hot damn, but he thought she was building toward another orgasm. He wanted to get her there before he gave in to the climax building for him.

He thrust again. He lifted her hips, positioning her so that his cock slid over her clit. When her nails bit into his shoulders, he knew she liked that—a lot. So he thrust again, gliding right over that sensitive spot even as he sank balls-deep into her.

She jerked beneath him, gasping out his name as she came. The contractions of her sex sent him right over the edge—over and into a volcano of pleasure. Hot, consuming, perfect. He shuddered and emptied himself in her.

When the pleasure finally started to wane—because those waves kept coming in slow bursts—he lifted his head. Her eyes were open. On him. So blue.

Once? He was supposed to be satisfied with one night with her?

No damn way.

CHAPTER FIVE

Clark Eastbridge didn't normally visit prisoners at night. He didn't normally pull strings to get special treatment. It just wasn't his way.

But this wasn't a normal situation.

He waited, his foot tapping a bit nervously, as the guard brought the prisoner to him.

The overhead lights glinted off Daniel Duvato's red hair. The guy was dressed in the usual orange prison garb, and a dark line of stubble covered Duvato's jaw. When he saw that Clark was waiting for him, the guy's eyes narrowed in fury.

"Not the freaking ADA again." Duvato jutted up his chin. "Not supposed to talk with you unless my lawyer is here!"

Right, that was the drill. And that was also why—

The door burst open. Phil Dunnway rushed into the room, suit rumpled, tie unknotted. "Don't say a word!" Phil blasted to his client. "If there's a deal on the table, I want to hear it."

Christ. Clark shook his head. "This is a courtesy visit, nothing more. Nothing less." It was a visit that he was already seriously regretting. But after that near accident with Sophie right outside of the courthouse, he'd just had to pay a visit to Duvato. "There's been a threat against you, Mr. Duvato."

The guy just laughed. Another asshole with a god complex. The fellow probably thought he was bulletproof, even in jail.

"A man has threatened to kill you, Mr. Duvato," Clark continued doggedly. "I wanted you to know—"

"I'm locked up!" A guard had shoved Daniel into the chair across from Clark. Daniel lifted his cuffed hands and pointed toward the guard. "I got these bozos around me twenty-four, seven. I don't think I have to worry about any threats."

Actually, he did. Jail hits were all too common. Anyone could be taken out, anywhere, if the price was right.

"Wait, wait!" Phil leaned forward, slapping his briefcase on the table in front of Duvato. "Is this threat credible? Is my client in danger?" He puffed up his chest. "Because if so, I want him moved to a new facility, immediately!"

Yes, he'd kind of thought that might be the guy's plan. "I don't know if the threat is credible yet."

Phil frowned. "Who made the threat?"

That was where this got interesting. With his gaze on Duvato, Clark said, "Sophie Sarantos was attacked last night."

Daniel leapt to his feet. The guard instantly shoved him back down. When his cuffed hands hit the table, they collided with Phil's briefcase. The briefcase tumbled off the edge of the table, and Phil hurried to collect the spilled contents.

Sophie's briefcase had spilled, too. Notes had been all across that road. But Sophie had been all right.

"A man broke into her home. He told her that he was going to kill you. Sophie reported the threat to me. She wanted to make sure you were safe." Which made no damn sense to him, considering that Duvato had tried to kill Sophie.

"Is she okay?" Duvato asked, and some of the hard bravado had actually left his face.

Clark could only shake his head. "You tried to kill her, and now you want to know if someone else hurt her?"

Duvato tried to rise again. And, again, the guard shoved him right back down.

"I liked Sophie. Always did," Duvato gritted out. "What I did…it had to be done. It was the only way to punish Ethan."

Right. Ethan Barclay. Clark held no love for that SOB. He'd been trying to nail the guy for crimes, hell, for years. But Barclay was too good at covering his tracks.

With Sophie's help, no doubt. He'd long suspected she and Ethan were lovers.

"The cop told me there would be no deal," Duvato said suddenly. "That lady detective…"

Faith Chestang. Yes, Clark knew her. She'd been the one to run lead on Duvato's case.

"But she's friends with Ethan. Another cop on the take with him. So she doesn't want to hear what I've got to say about my ex-boss." Duvato's eyes gleamed. "You want to hear what I got to say? Because I'd sure like to see him tossed into a cell right beside mine."

He hadn't come there for a deal. He'd gone there to give Duvato a warning. But now…*Maybe I can put that bastard Barclay away.* "I might be interested," Clark allowed.

Phil surged forward. "No! Not yet!" He held his briefcase in front of him like it was some kind of shield. "I have to speak with my client first. I need to know just what kind of evidence he's got. That way I can see—"

Clark waved his hand, cutting through Phil's words. "You want to see just what you can get. Well, here, I'll save you some trouble. I'll tell you what I want. I want enough evidence to convict Ethan Barclay—not for a year, not for two years." That just wouldn't cut it. "I want to make sure he won't be a threat to anyone else ever again, do you understand? So don't jerk me around. Give me something real, and in return, I'll try to make sure that the next twenty years aren't a complete living hell for Duvato."

Then Clark marched for the door. "I'll be back at nine a.m. Either you'll have evidence for me or there will never be talk of another deal again." Because he already had Duvato dead to rights, thanks to a confession the guy had given while in custody. But to get Ethan Barclay? Oh, hell, he might just bend a few rules.

"What about the threat?" Phil called after him.

Clark glanced back at the lawyer's question. "Is my client in danger?"

Clark turned his stare on Duvato. "You want extra guards?"

Duvato smiled. "They'll only get in my way."

Right. Whatever. He motioned to the officer on the other side of the door. The guy hurried and had him out in seconds. Clark was striding down the long corridor when Duvato's words finally sank in...

They'll only get in my way.

Those words didn't really make sense. Not unless...

Unless the bastard was planning something.

Clark stilled.

An escape attempt? Impossible. But...

Phil's briefcase had spilled. Duvato's hands had reached for that case. Had he grabbed some kind of weapon from it? Hell, to a desperate prisoner, even a pen could be a weapon. Jab it into your victim's neck and—

"Guards!" Clark bellowed as he whirled back toward the interrogation area. "Guards—secure the prisoner! Secure him now!"

The officer who'd just let Clark out was already rushing inside that little room.

But the sinking feeling in Clark's throat told him it was too late. He ran inside.

Blood. So much blood.

Phil was on the ground, twitching. The guard who'd led Duvato into interrogation was on the floor, too, his neck twisted at an unnatural angle, his body far too still.

Duvato was still leaning over Phil. The lawyer was alive—his chest shuddering and—

"Get away from him!" Clark bellowed.

The guard who'd rushed in right before Clark had frozen. The man's weapon was out, and Clark knew the guy was seconds away from shooting Duvato.

Duvato's right hand was fisted around what looked like—shit, it *was*—a bloody pen. A damn fountain pen. Clark looked down at Phil. The lawyer was shoving his fingers against the hole in his throat, a hole that still heavily pulsed blood.

"Told you…" Duvato said, "I don't need protection. I can take care of myself."

Shoot him. The words were on the tip of Clark's tongue. He knew he was staring at evil. At evil that had to be stopped. Only…

Duvato dropped the pen. "I still want that deal, ADA. I've got plenty to say to you about Ethan Barclay. Plenty." He laughed and he put his blood-covered hands up as more guards swarmed into the room.

He just killed a man. An officer of the law. And he thinks I'll still deal with him?

The world really would be better off with Daniel Duvato dead.

I should have given the fucking order.

***

When Sophie opened her eyes, Lex was beside her. His blond hair was mussed, tousled from her fingers, and his eyes were closed. He looked peaceful in sleep. But then, most people did. She was one of the few that nightmares always haunted.

Sunlight trickled through the curtains. Another day had come. But this was the first day she'd ever woken with a lover beside her. She didn't usually let anyone sleep with her because Sophie was just always worried. Afraid that she might let the wrong words slip during the night.

Thanks to Ethan, she'd learned that she talked in her sleep.

The things she said in sleep could incriminate her.

Another reason not to let a lover get too close. But Lex was close. So close that his arm was wrapped around her stomach even then. So close that her hip touched him. So close that she felt totally protected by his warmth and strength.

So close that she knew it was time she slipped away. So Sophie pulled in a careful breath and she began to inch to the left side of the bed, the side that promised freedom. She was completely naked and that just made her feel even more vulnerable. She'd slip away, go find the bag of clothes that they'd picked up from her place the night before, and then she'd face him feeling far more *normal.* She would—

"I don't want you to leave."

His eyes opened. There was none of the drowsy confusion that should have been present. He just opened his eyes and focused completely on her.

Unnerving.

Dammit, sexy. Why did she find so much about him to be sexy? Was it because he'd saved her life—twice? And now she had some kind of hero issue going on with him?

"You're even more beautiful first thing in the morning."

Okay, so maybe he had woken confused. She was sure her hair was a crazy tangle. And any makeup that she'd had on the day before would be long gone.

But he was still staring right at her and he made her feel beautiful in that moment. Part of her wanted to smile at him. To roll back toward him and sink fully into his embrace.

But her world didn't work like that. She'd given in to her need the night before. The day had dawned. "I need to get to work. I have clients who'll be waiting to see me today." Did she sound suitably in control?

In control. That was the role she always had to play. Even when she wanted to give up the mask, just for a little while.

Screw control.

She lifted his hand off her stomach. There were calluses on his fingers. She'd felt them when he caressed her last night. Those caresses had been so thorough. Inside and out.

She pretty much quivered thinking about some of them.

Lex definitely wasn't a selfish lover. The guy was so sensual. So fierce. So wonderfully focused.

He was probably the best lover she'd ever had.

"Running?" Lex asked her as she rolled from the bed. Sophie pulled the sheet with her, wrapping it around her body.

"No, just slowly walking…heading to the bathroom and then to find my clothes."

He sat up. Lex didn't seem to care that he was completely naked. With the sunlight hitting him, she saw the scars on his chest. White ridges. Red lines. From his time in the military?

Lex watched her, his gaze unfathomable. "Still don't trust me, do you?"

Not even a little bit. Well, maybe a little.

She turned and made her way to the bathroom. Her steps were a bit too fast for normal walking but being naked with Lex wasn't a good idea. Because when she was naked, when he was naked…she wanted to jump him.

Instead, she shut the bathroom door. Then she locked it. When she looked in the mirror, she didn't see her controlled image staring back at her. She saw a woman with eyes that were too big. Lips that were too red. Skin that was flushed.

She looked like she'd just had an amazing night.

She had.

And I didn't worry about being alone in the dark. Because I wasn't alone. I had Lex. I wasn't afraid. I just felt. So much pleasure.

He rapped on the door and Sophie jumped. Her right hand slapped against the countertop even as her left kept the sheet from falling to a puddle at her feet.

"Sophie?" Lex called out. "I brought your bag in for you."

Oh. That was nice. Thoughtful.

Not at all what a dangerous and wild lover would do.

Or was it? She'd never shared a morning after with the others so she wasn't real sure what they would have done.

Sophie opened the door. Lex stood there, her bag gripped in his hand. He lifted his brows at her. "It was your step two, right? Get to the bathroom, then get your clothes."

Her right hand grabbed for the bag. "Thank you."

He didn't move. "Sooner or later, I'll get you to trust me."

"Why?" She just didn't understand. "I'm paying you for the job, so nothing else really…"

Her voice trailed away.

Uh, oh. She could tell by the way his oh-so-muscled shoulders had just stiffened that she'd screwed up.

"Don't talk to me about payment." A muscle flexed in his hard jaw. "What happened between us last night had nothing to do with payment. It had *everything* to do with desire. With the freaking uncontrollable desire that I feel for you."

She had a death grip on her bag.

"And that you feel for me." His glittering gaze held her stare.

I do feel that desire for you.

"Get dressed, Sophie. Feel safer when you have your clothes on."

She, um, would.

"Then come find me. Because we've got a whole lot of talking to do." He spun on his heel. Took a step forward.

The light hit his back then. The pure sunlight. It fell on that powerful expanse and showed her all of the marks that he carried. Old marks…scars. They were faint white lines now, and, during the night, when it had been so dark, she'd never seen those marks. She hadn't felt them beneath her fingertips because they weren't raised. They were flat, smooth now from time.

And there were so many of them. Dozens.

She forgot about holding her sheet. Forgot about keeping her perfect mask of control. Her bag—and the sheet—fell as she lunged after him. Her trembling fingers touched his back.

Beaten. He was beaten. She knew exactly how he'd gotten those marks that covered so much of his back. "Who?" Sophie asked, her voice coming out angry and hard. These marks were so old. Had he gotten them when he was a child?

Her father had never left scars on her, not on the outside, anyway. He'd just liked to make her bones snap. Liked to twist until her wrist popped. Punch until a rib cracked. He'd—

Lex had gone completely still at her touch. But now, his head turned and he looked back at her. Anger flashed on his face, but then, as he stared at her, shock rippled across his expression. "Sophie…"

He turned toward her, and she made a mindless growl of anger.

"Sophie." He put his hand under her chin. "Are you crying for me?"

And she was. Sophie blinked, stunned to realize that her eyes had filled with tears. Those tears slid down her cheeks, cooling the flushed skin. The tears wouldn't stop. They just kept coming.

She didn't often cry for herself. But seeing that Lex had been hurt, that he'd been a victim, it had cut her right to the core.

"No, sweetheart, no." He wrapped his arms around her and pulled Sophie closer to him. "That was a long time ago."

Her breath was hitching. Her heart— breaking. "Who?"

His body stiffened, but his hold just tightened on her. "Who broke your bones? Who kept sending you to the hospital?"

She closed her eyes. "My father." And her mother hadn't stopped him. She'd just watched, with eyes that were weary. With a gaze long dead. *She watched.* Then, each time, when Sophie had come home from the hospital, her mother had sat on Sophie's bed. Voice sad, she'd said, "You shouldn't make him angry. I don't make him angry anymore. It's just you, Sophie. You have to stop being so bad. When the police come, don't be bad. Be a good girl."

A good girl didn't tell on her father. A good girl pretended she'd fallen again and again. At soccer practice. At ballet. In gym. Anywhere. Everywhere.

His hand stroked her hair. "My mother left me when I was just a baby. I never knew her. I think she was running away from him."

But she left you there?

"All of my memories of him..." Lex spoke softly and he kept stroking her hair. "They involve his fists or his belts. I know he had to be good. No one is always evil, right?"

Sophie wasn't so sure of that. Her tears still weren't stopping.

"The marks he left on me couldn't be explained away by a fall." Still, he stroked her hair, so carefully. "So when I was six, people came and they took me away from him."

People. Child services.

"I never saw the bastard again. I never wanted to see him."

When she closed her eyes, she saw her father. Not the enraged man he'd been, spittle flying from his mouth as he yelled at her.

But...her last image. Him on the floor, surrounded by a pool of blood. Her mother beside him, with that big hole between her eyes.

Sophie shuddered. "I'm sorry. I'm so sorry you were hurt."

"No one hurts me now."

She believed that.

"And no one will hurt you."

Her breath heaved out once more, then she pushed against his chest. His hold eased and she tipped back her head, staring up at him. She and Lex were far more alike than she'd originally realized. Survivors.

He'd grown from that past of pain and become a soldier. A protector. Not a monster.

And she…

Sophie wasn't sure what she was.

"The past only hurts us if we let it," Lex told her, voice gruff. "I buried that shit. It's not me, not anymore."

"I couldn't get away." Why was she telling him this? She'd never even told Ethan all the painful details. *As if not talking meant it didn't happen to me.* "I tried to run away — three times — but he'd find me each time. And when he brought me back home, he just hurt me more." Her right leg always ached in the evenings because she didn't think it had healed properly. "He'd keep me locked up, in the basement." That fucking basement that she hated. "And it was so dark there. If I screamed for help, he'd just come and hurt me again." Her words came, faster and faster. "He'd tell my friends I was sick. He'd send a note to the school. They all just thought I was ill. No one ever checked on me back then." No, that wasn't true. "Ethan would check. He fought with my father once."

"Sophie…"

"But when Ethan left, I had to pay the price." The tears were still coming, like a dam had been opened within her. "I asked him never to confront my dad again. I-I didn't think I'd survive if he did."

"Your father was one sick son of a bitch."

Yes. "He was a man who liked total control." No, more than that. "He was a twisted bastard who enjoyed hurting those who were weaker." First her mother, and then, when Sophie had come along…*me.*

She kept her gaze on Lex. "You aren't anything like your father." She'd never felt fear of Lex. Sure, he had plenty of power, but when she was with him, she felt protected. Safe. Not threatened.

"And you're nothing like yours."

A sob broke from her.

"Sophie, you are tearing out my heart." He pulled her close again and pressed a kiss to her forehead. "What can I do to make it better? What can I do?"

Nothing. Because her monster was dead. And his was in the past.

She wrapped her arms around him. "I wish I could take away the pain you had." He was such a good man, at his core. He hadn't deserved what happened to him.

"Sweetheart, I'd give my soul to take away yours."

Her heart stopped. He actually sounded as if he meant those words. Impossible, of course, but—

A loud pounding echoed through the house.

"What the hell?" Lex muttered and he pulled away. "Sounds like someone's at the front door."

She felt cold, too exposed, as he hurried toward the bedroom door. Sophie grabbed the sheet, needing it now.

Lex jerked on a pair of jeans. "Stay here, Sophie. I'll take care of this." He hurried from the room.

Who could be at his door that early? Dev? His other partner, Chance Valentine? She swiped her hand over her face, trying to get rid of those tears. She felt hollowed out on the inside, her heart raw, her emotions all over the place. This just wouldn't do. She never broke apart. She couldn't afford to do it.

But seeing the scars on Lex's back, realizing that he'd been a victim, just as she had…that had changed everything for her. Lex wasn't someone to be used and discarded. He was so much more.

"What are you doing here?" Lex's angry voice carried easily to her because he'd left the bedroom door open.

"I need to see Sophie." And that voice — a voice just as angry, just as deep — it had her stumbling toward the bedroom door. *Ethan Barclay.* If Ethan had tracked her to Lex's place, then that could *not* be a good sign.

"Too fucking bad," Lex snarled back. "Sophie is busy right now."

Crap. She needed clothes, right then. Her frantic gaze flew around the room. Where had she dropped that bag?

"So why don't you just haul your ass out," Lex's fierce voice continued. "And I'll get her to call you later." Then he swore. "Hell, how did you even find my place? How did you know she was with me?"

Based on that lethal tone, she didn't have time to dress. She kept that sheet around her and sprinted through the bedroom door.

"I know *everything* about Sophie," Ethan said, his voice far too knowing.

She ran down the hallway. She could see those two men — big, fierce, and looking as if they were about to come to blows at any second.

"Not everything," Lex threw right back.

No, Ethan didn't know everything, but he thought he did.

"You slept with her, huh?" Ethan drawled. "Then I guess she's done with you now."

Lex surged toward Ethan. Ethan jumped right toward Lex.

"Stop!" Sophie yelled. They stilled.

She kept running until she was close enough to grab Ethan's arm. Then she jerked him away from Lex and toward her. "What are you doing here?"

His golden eyes — only Ethan had eyes that color — glared down at her. "I was worried about you. You weren't home. I heard buzz about an attack..." His hands closed around her shoulders. "You should have come to me."

Once, Ethan's face had been eerily close to perfect. *Before* Daniel Duvato got hold of him. Now, Ethan's high cheekbones were marked. A long, still angry red scar went down his left cheek and another sliced down his right. His dark hair was longer than before, and it looked as if he'd been running his fingers through the tousled mane.

"She came to me," Lex said, stepping forward. "Now get your hands off her."

Ethan didn't. She knew Ethan wasn't used to following orders.

"Get. Them. Off." Lex advanced more, closing the last of the distance between them. "You're in my house, asshole, and Sophie is—"

Ethan dropped his hands and turned to face Lex. "What? She's yours?" He laughed, the sound mocking. "Don't kid yourself. It's obvious Sophie had her fun with you, but I know her. She's done now." He inclined his head toward Sophie. "Let's go. We have things to discuss in private."

Ethan had been her best friend for more years than she could count. Her confidant. She knew the world saw him as some kind of villain, and sure, the guy wasn't always on the side of the law abiding, but…

He loves me. She knew that with certainty. She was Ethan's only family, just as he was hers.

He'd paid for her college. Her law school. He'd gotten her away from the nightmare of her past.

But she wasn't leaving with him.

Her gaze slid to Lex. Lex wasn't staring at Ethan any longer. Lex's green stare was on her. He was waiting. Waiting for her to make a choice?

She'd made that choice. "I'm not done." She should have said something more profound. Lex's gaze had just widened. Hell. Was she screwing this up? "I'm with Lex." *I'm with Lex.* Why did that feel so right to say?

"What?" And Ethan reached out to her again. "Sophie—"

Just that fast—a blink—Lex had Ethan across the room and pinned against the wall. Lex's arm was locked under Ethan's jaw as he said, "I told you…don't touch her. I get that you two are friends. Maybe even some kind of screwed-up family. But Sophie is naked under that sheet and when you get close to her, when you get all handsy, it really pisses me off."

She pulled the sheet up a bit.

"Didn't think I was the jealous sort," Lex continued, his voice still that rough tangle of fury and possession. "Until her."

Ethan wasn't fighting, a surprise there. Because she knew he could be a vicious fighter.

And I have no doubt that Lex can be, too. She didn't want to see what would happen if those two ever really did go after each other. Right then, Lex was just holding Ethan back.

"Get something straight," Lex demanded as he kept his focus on Ethan. "Sophie is mine. She came to me when the shit got bad in her life. Me, not you. And I'll do anything she wants. *Anything.*"

Sophie inched forward. "Don't hurt him." She wasn't sure if that warning was for Ethan or for Lex.

Ethan must have thought the warning was for him. "Loverboy…" Ethan ground out, "is the one choking me."

Sophie put her hand on Lex's shoulder. "Let him go."

He immediately did. Then Lex swung to her. "If you want me sane, please just put on some damn clothes around him. You being naked with him isn't going to fucking fly with me near. It's not going to fly, period."

He really was jealous. She didn't feel some sort of power surge with that knowledge. She just shook her head. "It's never been like that with us. It never will be." She turned from him. Then Sophie realized something important. What she'd felt with Lex the night before, *it had never been like that with anyone*. Her heart was beating too fast as she said, "Don't kill each other while I dress, got it? I'll be right back."

Then Sophie ran down that hallway as fast as she could.

They might not kill each other before she got back. But hurting each other? That could be a definite possibility.

CHAPTER SIX

He didn't lunge at Ethan again. Lex was rather proud of his restraint, but he did glare at the asshole. He'd first met Ethan when VJS had been hired to protect Gwen Hawthorne. Pretty Gwen had picked up a very dangerous stalker—and all signs had pointed to that stalker being her ex-lover, Ethan Barclay. With Ethan's shady reputation, it had been easy enough to imagine the fellow as the bad guy.

And Chance Valentine, well, he sure as hell hadn't been keen on Ethan. Chance didn't like it for any other man to get too close to Gwen.

Now I understand how he feels. I probably shouldn't have given him such a hard time about the way he was twisted in knots over Gwen. I'm just as twisted up for Sophie.

Maybe even more so.

"So...are you planning to glare at me all day?" Ethan asked as he rolled back his shoulders.

"Not all day. Just until Sophie comes back."
He gave Ethan a grim smile. "She went to our
bedroom to dress."

Ethan didn't take the bait and come at him to
attack. The guy just laughed. Annoying, mocking
laughter. Then Ethan said, "The fact that she slept
with you means you *don't* matter, man. Get that
in your head. You're one and done with her."

His spine snapped up. "You have no clue, do
you? Not about her, not really." She'd cried in his
arms and Sophie had broken something in him
with her tears. He was different now, he could
feel it.

"I know plenty about Sophie." Ethan's gaze
measured him. "But what I don't know…that's
you. Why are you pushing so hard to get close to
Sophie?"

Was the guy serious? Sophie was beautiful,
smart, determined —

"Is this because you and your jerk buddies at
VJS want to take me down? Are you still gunning
for me after all?"

Ethan was delusional.

"I never hurt Gwen," Ethan continued, "so
you damn well better not have plans to hurt
Sophie."

He didn't lunge at the guy. Didn't shove his
forearm against Ethan's throat again. But Lex
could feel the fury pouring through him.

"Hurting Sophie is the last thing I intend. I told you already, she came to me."

"And Sophie always comes to me!" Now Ethan was almost yelling as his control fractured. "I'm the one there for her! The one she can count on, the one—"

"Not this time." Just saying those words filled Lex with a savage satisfaction. Whatever Sophie and Ethan had, this time… "She came to me."

Ethan's golden eyes glittered. "Sophie—"

"—is back," Sophie called as she hurried into the room. She was bouncing a bit as she tried to shove on one of her high heels. The woman had dressed in real record time. Her hair tumbled over her shoulders and her face—free of makeup—was gorgeous. But…

He could see the faint tear marks on her cheeks.

Ethan was frowning at her now. Seeming to get a real look at Sophie. The guy stalked forward and his eyes narrowed on her face. "What did he do?" Before, Ethan's voice had been hard with fury. Now, it was soft. Deadly. "Just tell me, and I'll make it all better."

Alarm flashed on Sophie's face, then her hands immediately rose to scrub her cheeks. "Nothing! No, Lex didn't do anything to me!"

Giving a guttural growl, Ethan whirled to face Lex.

But Sophie grabbed his arm and yanked him back toward her. "*Nothing!*" Sophie said again. "Look, I hired him to protect me, all right?"

So much for keeping that secret. Maybe she *didn't* keep anything from Ethan.

That jealousy was back, pouring like acid through Lex's veins.

"Someone broke into my home," Sophie said. She was still holding onto Ethan's arm. "A jerk with a knife. He said that he was there to make sure I was all right, but I didn't buy that bull."

"Because of the fucking knife." Ethan's voice was still that quiet menace.

"He told me that he was going to kill Daniel Duvato."

Ethan blinked.

"I couldn't come to you. I-I was worried..." Her voice dropped and her hand slipped away from Ethan. "About what you might do."

"Sophie..."

"Lex is working on this case." She nodded firmly. "He's got this. VJS has this."

Lex rather liked the confident way she said that.

"You don't have to swoop in for the rescue, Ethan. I'm okay."

Damn straight she was.

But Lex noticed that Sophie hadn't mentioned the near accident in front of the courthouse. Since she didn't mention it, neither did he. He wanted Sophie to know he could keep her secrets, too.

"I didn't come here to rush to your rescue." Ethan's lips thinned. "I need you to come to mine."

"What?" When Sophie shook her head, her hair slid over her shoulders in a gleaming black curtain.

"Daniel Duvato," Ethan spat out that name. "He's fucking trouble that I should have ended long ago."

Lex's stare drifted between them. He was pretty sure Ethan had just threatened to kill Daniel.

"A cop who owes me…that cop let me know that Daniel is planning to make a deal with the ADA. Seems they had a chat last night, and Daniel wants to see me locked in a cell right next to his."

"That's not happening," Sophie said immediately.

Lex kept quiet, just listening and taking in as much as he could.

"I don't know what kind of evidence the guy *thinks* he has on me—"

"He worked with you for years," Sophie said.

Years of secrets. Of crimes?

Sophie's gaze cut to Lex. She blinked and a mask seemed to fall, veiling some of the brilliance of her eyes. "Ethan is my client."

Lex was sure that been handy in the past, especially if Sophie saw Ethan's less-than-legal activities.

Sophie gave a quick nod. "I need to get down to the station right away. I'll talk with Clark and figure out just what the hell is going on." She started a determined stride toward the door.

Lex stepped in her path. "You mean *we'll* be going down there."

"Lex—"

"What are you planning, Sophie? A little sit-down with Daniel Duvato?" He threw that out there because suspicion had knotted his gut.

She didn't so much as blink. "If necessary. No deal will be made. Ethan isn't going to be incriminated."

"Then maybe Ethan shouldn't have broken the damn law!"

She flinched.

"Watch it," Ethan warned softly. "I get real particular about the way people speak to Sophie."

Lex turned his head and met the guy's glare with his own fury. "And I get real particular about people putting her in danger. Daniel tried to kill her and you! So what, you just expect Sophie to go in there and have a little friendly chat with the guy? Show him the error of his ways?"

"I'll handle Daniel," Ethan said confidently. "I just need Sophie to take care of the ADA. Convince the guy that Daniel is just spouting bullshit."

Lex's temples were throbbing. "Sophie, seriously, this is a bad idea."

"I have to do my job." She held his stare a moment longer, then glanced toward Ethan. "Don't say anything else in front of Lex. You're my client. He has no ties to you at all."

The woman was telling Ethan to shut the hell up before he incriminated himself. *Too late, sweetheart.* Lex had already realized that Ethan was a killer.

He'd put all of the pieces together. The fierce way Sophie protected the guy. The bond that was so strong between them. Sophie's father had hurt her, over and over, and that abuse had only stopped once the man was dead.

Lex knew exactly who'd killed Sophie's father. The cops might not have a clue, but he knew. He suspected that Daniel Duvato did, too.

Ethan Barclay had saved Sophie from her nightmare, and Lex realized that—now—Sophie was determined to protect the other man, at all costs.

***

Sophie had been at the police station more times than she could count. Some days, the trips there were to talk with cops—informants that she had carefully cultivated on the force. Other days, she was there to sit in on interrogations as she did her best to protect her clients.

Today, she was there for one very basic reason.

To save Ethan's ass.

Lex was at her side. He'd insisted on traveling with her, and she had to admit, she was glad he was there. After that near run-in with the black SUV the night before, having a bodyguard at her side really eased the fear.

"I guess you heard about last night…"

At that feminine voice, Sophie glanced to the right and found Detective Faith Chestang strolling toward her. Faith was smart with a hard-edge that Sophie respected. The two women didn't always see eye-to-eye, mostly because Faith was usually trying to get Sophie's clients locked up, but the lady was a good cop.

Faith's skin was a warm caramel, her hair a perfect black. She was pretty, but Sophie knew that Faith tried to downplay her looks at the police station. Like that was going to work. Sophie used the opposite tactic. She tried to let her looks distract as much as possible. If men didn't take her seriously enough, that was their own idiotic fault. It made moving in for the kill so much easier.

"Last night?" Sophie repeated carefully. She often liked to let the cops talk first because they tended to overshare that way.

Faith nodded grimly. Her gaze slid to Lex, then back to Sophie. "When Daniel Duvato killed a guard and drove a fountain pen into his lawyer's throat."

Lex swore.

Sophie rocked back on her heels. "No, no, I didn't hear about that." She was suddenly very glad that she'd convinced Ethan to wait outside. If he'd busted in there with her and heard this news… *Or does he already know? Is that the real reason he came looking for me?* "I'd been told only that Duvato and Clark Eastbridge were talking about a deal, a deal that might impact my client, Ethan Barclay."

Faith glanced away. "I might've heard that too."

And had she been the one to tip off Ethan? Sophie hadn't thought that Faith and Ethan were close, but maybe Ethan had been holding back on her.

Faith shrugged her shoulders as her gaze slowly returned to Sophie. "They were having a little deal talk last night, right before Duvato showed the ADA just how much of a menace the guy is." She shook her head. "The ADA is crazy on this one. No one should offer Duvato a deal. The guy needs to stay locked up forever." Her head cocked as she studied Sophie. "I'm sure you, of all people, feel the same way."

She'd tried to style her hair during the ride over. Worked to make it look like less of a night-after-tangle. She'd also used her hair to hide the scar that Daniel Duvato had given to her when he smashed a lamp over her head. "I think Daniel has nothing useful to offer anyone. A swift trial and a trip to a maximum security prison should be the only thing in his future."

Faith pointed down the hallway. "Instead of maximum security, he's in holding back there. Two officers are with him. He's cuffed, hands and feet. The bastard isn't going to be making another attempt to hurt anyone."

Good. That was good.

"Where's Clark?" Sophie asked. She had to stop him from going in that room and talking with Duvato. Or at least, she had to convince him that anything Duvato said was total bull.

"He's with Duvato now."

Dammit, no. "Then so am I."

Lex grabbed her arm. "Sophie…"

She tossed back her hair. Tried to look like she had this situation totally under control. "I have a client to protect." Surely he didn't notice that her knees were shaking.

He leaned in close. "And I want to protect you."

The last thing she wanted to do was go in that holding area. "I'll be right back," she promised.

"Sophie…"

She pulled away from him. Her heels clicked on the tiled floor. Her knees were still shaking.

***

"I think that woman might have balls of steel," Faith said as she turned her head and watched Sophie stride away.

She's got a protective streak. She's doing this for Barclay. Right then, Lex could have cheerfully beat the hell out of that guy. "I want back there, Faith."

She laughed. "Right. Cause you're a cop and all…"

"Come on, get me back there. Into an observation room. We both know there's one back there. I just need to be close to her."

Her face held a bit of suspicion as she studied him. "I heard about that hit and run last night outside of the courtroom. I also heard that—all of a sudden—you two are real close."

He stared back at her.

"Bodyguard?"

He didn't confirm or deny.

"I told her she should get someone to watch after her. Glad she listened to me."

So was he.

She crept a bit closer. "If I do this, VJS totally owes me. And so does Ethan. Make sure he knows that. I'll be calling in these debts."

He knew she would, but Faith wouldn't want money. She'd never been on the take. Never had, never would be. In her business, knowledge was power. VJS and Ethan Barclay had plenty of knowledge to give her. Contacts that she could use.

He nodded.

"Then come this way because I wanted to keep my eyes on that bastard, too."

***

"Clark." Sophie had just thrown open the door to that holding room. The cop outside had let her march right in—he knew her well. *A handy contact.*

Clark's head jerked up at her voice. "Sophie, what are you doing here?"

"Sophie…" Daniel jumped to his feet. "Sophie, I'm sorry."

What? She turned her furious stare on him. Daniel was dressed in garish orange, and the wanna-be beard that he was growing looked like shit. "Sorry? For trying to kill me? And Ethan? For killing his fiancée? For—"

"For hurting you," Daniel said, his shoulders slumping. "You're the only part I regret."

This was insane. No, Daniel was insane.

"You'd been hurt enough," he added.

Her chin shot up. "Clark, I need to talk with you outside. Right now."

Clark was already closing in on her. "You can't be in here. The cops should *never* have let you inside. This is private, against every code—"

"He killed a guard last night. Attacked his lawyer. And you know what? I bet Daniel doesn't care that I'm here at all. Do you, Daniel?" Sophie challenged, raising her voice.

"You can be my lawyer, Soph," Daniel shouted back. Two guards were shoving him back into his seat. "You can hear everything I've got to say about Ethan!"

No one would hear what he had to say.

She glanced at the uniformed cops holding him. One met her stare, the guy on the right—the one with dark brown hair and a hard hazel gaze. Their eyes met for a brief moment, a moment when she saw his rage—rage directed at the prisoner he held so tightly. Sophie nodded. That cop would do his job.

This is what happens when you kill one of their own. You piss them off. You stir a killing fury.

Clark pushed her from the room. One of the uniformed cops followed them out, but the one with the rage in his gaze—he stayed inside.

Good choice.

The door shut behind them with a clang. "What the hell, Sophie? What are you doing?"

"Protecting my client."

"Barclay." Disgust was in the name.

"Duvato is spouting lies to you. You can't believe anything that man says. He's a killer, nothing more. *Nothing more.*"

CHAPTER SEVEN

Lex didn't make it to the observation room. When he rounded the corner heading toward that room, he saw the ADA and Sophie locked in a heated conversation. They were in the middle of the hallway and—

"Barclay is a killer, too!" Clark blasted.

"So what, you make a deal with one devil to catch another?"

Clark turned away, seemingly about to head back into the holding room. "If necessary."

Sophie grabbed him and jerked the guy toward her. "It's not necessary. Daniel Duvato is scum. He's full of lies, and I won't let him impinge my client—"

Thunder came then, blasting hard. Lex lunged forward even as Faith drew her own weapon because he knew that blast wasn't really thunder—it was gunfire and it had come from *inside* that holding room.

Before he could reach Sophie, Clark had grabbed her and pulled her away from the holding area, wrapping his arms around her as if he'd shield her.

"Sophie!" Lex reached for her and Clark looked up, his face tight and his eyes wild.

"Bastard killed one guard last night," Clark bit out. "Not again…"

Faith and another officer kicked open the door to the holding room. They raced inside. Lex pulled Sophie toward him, making sure his body was the one protecting her. But when he looked into that holding room, Daniel Duvato wasn't brandishing a weapon. He was on the floor, his body twitching, as blood flowed from the wound in his chest.

A dark-haired officer stood over him. "He went for my weapon," the guy said. He didn't take his gaze off Daniel. "I wasn't about to end up the way prison guard Charlie Branson did. Murdered by this SOB."

"Get a medic!" Faith yelled as she crouched near Daniel.

A medic wasn't going to do the guy much good.

"S-Sophie…" A desperate croak that was her name—Daniel's voice strained as he tried to call out to her in what Lex knew were the guy's last moments.

He hoped Sophie hadn't heard that call.

But she pushed against his chest. Her head lifted. "He wants me."

Too bad. The guy was dying. He'd never have the chance to attack her—

Sophie pushed against Lex again. He just tightened his hold on her. More cops were swarming back there, and he wanted to get Sophie out of there.

"I have to see him." Her voice was fierce. "I have to."

Dammit. He let her go.

Clark had rushed back into the holding room. Lex saw that Clark had taken the gun away from the officer who'd fired—the cop was a tall fellow, a little on the thin side, with close-cropped brown hair. He looked pretty young, maybe in his early twenties. When Lex looked up at the fellow's eyes, he expected to see shock. Maybe horror.

No emotion was there.

"S-Sophie…"

Daniel was still alive. Fighting to keep talking. Sophie tried to get closer to him.

Lex caught her hand in his. "That's close enough." Then he raised his voice. "She's here, Daniel. Say whatever the hell it is—"

"S-sorry, Soph…" Daniel's breath rattled in his lungs. Rattled—

Silence.

Daniel Duvato wouldn't be a threat to anyone else ever again.

***

He watched as Sophie was led out of the police station. She kept glancing over her shoulder, looking back as if she couldn't quite believe what had just happened.

Daniel Duvato is dead. Just like I promised you.

He'd just needed to put the right amount of money into the right hand. It had been so easy. Sure, he would've liked to pull the trigger himself, but dead was dead.

Sophie stood on the station's steps. Her new lover was at her side. The lover wrapped his arm around her shoulder as he tried to act all protective. Such bullshit. Sophie didn't need anyone protecting her.

That's what I'm here for.

He was looking out for Sophie. Protecting her, as no one else could. He wasn't afraid to make the tough choices. Wasn't afraid for lives to be lost. Those who hurt Sophie got exactly what they deserved.

Pain. Death.

Did she realize it was all for her? He hoped so. Maybe he'd visit her again. Let her show her appreciation to him. With Daniel soon to be rotting in the ground, he knew Sophie would be happy.

Would she kiss him when he went to her?

Wrap her arms around him and hold him tight?

He couldn't wait to see just how much Sophie appreciated all he'd done for her.

***

Ethan Barclay was running toward them.

Talk about some seriously bad timing. When the guy rushed up the police station's steps, Lex put out his hand. "You need to get the hell out of here," he ordered.

Ethan ignored him and stared at Sophie's too pale face. Lex didn't like that pallor.

"What happened, Sophie?" Ethan seemed to brace himself. "Were you too late? Did Daniel talk?"

Lex glanced over his shoulder. He could practically feel eyes on them. "Daniel isn't talking to anyone right now. Seriously, man, get the hell out of here. We'll call you." He started ushering Sophie down the steps.

Ethan followed.

"He's dead," Sophie whispered. "One of the guards—it was Griffin Hollister, the new guy—Griffin shot Daniel. Daniel was reaching for his weapon. Griffin had to defend himself." Her words were stilted, almost as if she were speaking on some kind of autopilot, and she definitely sounded like she was channeling her inner defense attorney.

Ethan stopped following them. "Dead?"

He sounded satisfied. Lex didn't have time to deal with his shit right then. He kept going. Lex hit the sidewalk and just hurried faster until he had Sophie safely in his car. "I'm glad he's dead." Her voice was quiet. "Is that wrong?"

He cranked the car and pulled away as fast as he could. "Daniel left you unconscious in a house filling with gas. He left you to die. I don't know that there's a whole lot *right* with that situation." He risked a fast glance at Sophie and found her staring down at her hands. She'd fisted them in her lap.

"I was glad when my father was dead, too."

He braked at a red light. "Sophie…" He just wanted to pull her into his arms.

She looked up at him. There were no tears in her eyes. No rage. *Just like the guard.* Maybe Sophie was in shock. Violence and death could drive a person too far.

"I should have been sorry about my mother. She hadn't hurt me." She bit her lip. "I think something is wrong with me," Sophie confessed. "I don't feel the way I should."

The light changed. He shoved the gas pedal down against the floor board. "There isn't a fucking thing wrong with you."

"I should feel something. *Something.* A man died in front of me, and all I have is this relief… " Her voice trailed away.

"He tried to kill you! The guy was a sadistic murderer! So what if you don't shed tears for him?" There was nothing wrong with her. As far as he was concerned, she was everything right in his world.

But he could practically feel her slipping away from him. His right hand reached out and grabbed her left hand. Held tight. "Nothing is wrong," he said again, needing her to believe him.

Sophie was too stiff, not responding. Okay. He needed to get them off that road and into a safe place, pronto. Luckily VJS Protection was just minutes away. At the next intersection, he took a hard right. Horns followed him, but Lex didn't care.

He drove faster. Lex spun into the parking garage when he finally reached his destination, and then he hauled ass up the elevator with her.

She didn't look at him in the elevator. She didn't seem to be looking at anything.

"Sophie." He touched her cheek. "Don't do this. Don't freeze me out."

Lex thought he saw her lower lip tremble.

"I'm no good for you," Sophie said. "I should have handled all this on my own. You're too close."

Damn straight he was close, and he planned to get closer. "You think I haven't seen this before? On the battlefield, it happened too many times."

"I'm not on the battlefield," Sophie whispered as she closed her eyes. "I'm not a soldier."

"You're in shock."

"No, I'm—"

"You're shutting down to protect yourself because you don't want any more pain. Daniel Duvato was your friend, wasn't he, Sophie? For years, he worked with Ethan, so that meant he worked with you. You knew him, and you trusted him, didn't you?"

Her eyes were still closed.

"Then he turned on you and shattered that trust."

"It's not safe to trust anyone," she said, her voice husky.

"It's safe to trust me, sweetheart. I won't let you down." He leaned over her and pressed a soft kiss to her lips. "I swear it."

Her eyes fluttered open. She gazed at him, her expression stark. "He *was* my friend, before he tried to kill me."

"And it was your *friend* that you saw on that floor, bleeding out, wasn't it?" The elevator had stopped. He heard the doors open behind him, but Lex didn't move. "It was your *friend* telling you he was sorry as he lay dying."

He heard her breath hitch. "We spent holidays together. Summers…one year, he tried to surf down in Miami and no matter what he did, Daniel just couldn't stand on that surfboard. He crashed about a dozen times before he gave up."

Daniel Duvato had been a twisted, cold-blooded killer. Once, though, he'd been something more.

"You don't have to shut yourself off," Lex told her. "Sweetheart, I'm right here."

Her gaze searched his.

He could read her so well right then. It was almost as if she thought that if she let her emotions out, she'd never be able to control them again. "I'll take care of you."

Sophie pulled in a deep breath. "I—"

"*Lex.*"

That was Chance's voice. Coming from right behind him. Lex turned and saw that Chance Valentine stood on the edge of the elevator. Chance had thrown out a hand to stop the elevator doors from closing again. Chance's dark eyes swept over Lex—and Sophie. "We need to talk," Chance said flatly.

He didn't want to talk with Chance right then. He wanted to stay with Sophie. She needed him and—

"There's intel you don't know," Chance said. "We *need* to talk. Now." His face was hard.

Sophie pushed against Lex. "If this is intel about me, then shouldn't I be in this little meeting?"

And, just like that, Lex had lost her. He could practically see Sophie putting her walls back in place. How many years had she done that? Tried to block herself off from others? She was wrong about herself not feeling. Actually, Lex thought she might feel too much.

"Of course," Chance said, inclining his head toward her. "Why don't you both just come into my office…"

Lex didn't want to go in there. He wanted Sophie in *his* office where they could be alone. Hell, he hadn't even thought that Chance would be in at VJS. He'd just known the place was close, and he'd wanted it to be a safe haven for Sophie.

Sophie slipped by Lex. He shook his head and followed her. Chance led their little group, taking them down the narrow hallway, past their receptionist, and into Chance's office. The guy had a killer view—a view very similar to Lex's own. Big windows looked out over DC, showing them the capital's skyline.

"You were both on scene when Daniel Duvato died," Chance began as soon as Lex shut the door.

Lex's brows shot up in surprise. His buddy had sure learned that news fast.

Chance's lips quirked, but the smile didn't reach his eyes. "I've got friends down at the station." He motioned to the chair near his desk. "Sophie, why don't you have a seat?"

She slipped into the chair. Crossed her legs. Lex's gaze dipped to her heels, then slid back to her face.

Don't lock yourself away, Sophie.

Lex didn't sit, but he did march closer to her. He propped his shoulders against the wall, crossed his arms over his chest, and waited.

"Your stalker told you that he'd kill Daniel Duvato," Chance said. Lex had fully briefed Chance and Dev on everything that bastard had said to her. "And now Daniel is on his way to the morgue."

"He attacked an officer who'd been assigned to guard him. The officer fired in self-defense." Her words were too calm. "That's not my stalker. That's just life." She shook her head. "And death. Maybe Daniel had a death wish. Maybe he thought he was invincible. I don't know, but, yes, he's gone now."

Chance glanced over at Lex. "Did you talk to the guard?" He looked back at his desk, picked up a notepad, and said, "Griffin Hollister?"

"There wasn't time for a chat," Lex said, wondering where this was going. "The ADA had him and the cops were swarming. My priority was to get Sophie out of there."

Sophie shifted in her seat. "Daniel killed a guard last night. Griffin told us all that he wasn't about to wind up the same way. Perhaps he was a little trigger happy, but given the circumstances—"

"You *knew* Griffin," Chance cut in. "Didn't you, Sophie?"

"What? Well, yes. I'd see him a few times, with other prisoners—some clients."

"And your buddy Ethan knows him, too, right?"

Because Lex was watching Sophie so carefully, he saw the faint flutter of her lashes. "I wouldn't know."

She's lying. Now Lex stood a little straighter, gaze focused and body on alert.

"When Ethan was… ah…in police custody a while back," Chance said, "Griffin was one of his guards."

"I don't remember that."

"He was. My friends at the PD told me."

This shit is getting tangled. What had seemed like simple self-defense such a short time ago now felt a whole lot more sinister.

Sophie's heel slowly kicked back and forth. "You've got some helpful friends."

Chance tilted his head as he studied her. "It's interesting that Daniel was at the police station today, I mean, he wasn't being held at the station before. That's not standard. He was brought in, though, and you were conveniently there for that little meeting this morning."

Her heel kept swinging. "I was there because he was trying to make a deal with the ADA. He wanted to implicate my client in crimes—"

"Your client..." Chance rubbed his chin and propped his hip against the edge of the desk. The guy looked relaxed, but Lex knew that image was a lie. "You mean Ethan Barclay."

"We all know who she means," Lex muttered darkly.

Sophie didn't look ruffled. Her emotions were all still locked up. "If you know everything, then why are you asking me questions?"

Lex was thinking the same thing. He also was thinking he didn't like the way Chance was pushing Sophie. Friend or no friend, that shit was about to stop. "Chance..." His voice held a warning note.

Chance smiled. "Ethan Barclay once told me that he had friends in prison and that maybe Daniel wouldn't survive long." He paused. "I guess he was right about that, huh?"

Sophie slowly stood. "If you have an accusation—"

"Ethan Barclay was also at the police station today, wasn't he?" Chance's gaze swung to Lex.

Lex gave a grim nod. "Yeah, he was there." But he'd been waiting outside. Ethan had been nowhere near Daniel when the guy was shot.

Chance cut his gaze back to Sophie. "And, conveniently, before he could roll on your *client*, Daniel was taken out."

"A cop shot him—" Lex began.

"A cop that Dev has already linked to Ethan. Griffin Hollister has been going to Ethan's club, Wicked, for the last two weeks. He's a new regular there. And one of Ethan's enemies has been eliminated. Ethan's enemy...and yours, Ms. Sarantos."

"This is ridiculous," Sophie announced. "I don't have to listen to you accuse my friend of taking out some kind of hit!" Sophie stood and swung toward Lex. "This is why you brought me here? I thought..." She gave a sharp, negative shake of her head. "Forget what I thought." She strode toward the door.

Lex caught her quickly, catching her wrist in his grasp. "Wait, Sophie, just wait." He tossed a hot glare at Chance. "So you're telling us that Ethan Barclay arranged for that hit? He let it go down right in front of Sophie?"

"Actually, I'm wondering..." Chance's expression tightened. "Were Sophie and Ethan in on the plan together? Because I've got to imagine that they both wanted Duvato dead." Chance obviously wasn't backing down. "And since I am such a suspicious bastard, I can't help but think that this whole case has been a run of perfect circumstances." He held up his hand and started counting off the circumstances. "A man breaks into Sophie's house and he threatens Sophie. Well, after that, she just had to go to the ADA with that threat, right?"

"Stop," Sophie said, but she didn't look at Chance. She kept her eyes on Lex.

Chance didn't stop. "And the ADA, well, he had to go and see Daniel Duvato. While he was there, of course, Duvato pushed for a deal. Offered to give up the goods on Ethan. We all knew that would happen, right? Considering how much Daniel hated Ethan. Easy enough to predict."

"You can't predict anything with Daniel," Sophie said as she stared up at Lex. "That's why another guard died last night and Daniel's lawyer is in intensive care."

"I don't know." Now Chance was musing. "I think a woman who knows criminals as well as you do, I think a woman like you might be able to predict that the ADA would move Daniel to the station—and that would put him within reach of Griffin, right?"

She whirled to face Chance. "You have a great imagination."

He shrugged. "It's a gift."

Lex growled. He was pissed at Chance but something was nagging at him. Something about the shooting at the station.

"For the hit to go down, there couldn't be witnesses, though. So maybe that was where you came in. Your job was to get the ADA out of that room. You distracted the ADA, and Griffin made the hit." Chance slapped his hands together. "And just like that, a threat is eliminated from your life and from Ethan's."

"A great imagination," Sophie said again. "But that's all it is...imagination."

A knock sounded on the door.

"Come in, Dev," Chance called.

Lex looked over and saw Dev head into the office. Dev's face was far too grim. *This isn't going to be good.* Nothing about the trip to VJS had been good so far.

"You accessed Griffin's bank records?" Chance asked.

Oh, hell.

Dev nodded. "Twenty grand was deposited into Griffin's account two days ago."

"What?" The surprise in Sophie's voice seemed real.

"Two days. That sure is real close to the time of that little visit you got from your stalker," Chance pointed out.

Sophie marched toward Dev. "That twenty grand you found...where did it come from?"

"I'm still tracking it. Right now, I just know there was a payoff."

She swallowed. Lex saw the delicate movement of her throat. Her gaze came to him, then darted to Chance, and finally back to Dev. "So that's it. You all think I've been tricking you? Using VJS as what—some kind of cover? That the plan all along was to move Daniel out into a more accessible spot to off him?" She smiled. It was grim. Cold. "A good plan. But not my plan."

"Was it Ethan's?" Chance asked.

She sighed. "You are so hung up on him being the bad guy. Why? Because he had sex with your precious Gwen? Don't get me wrong, I like Gwen, but jealousy can make a man go blind. In this case, you're blind. Ethan didn't do this. I didn't do this." She flashed her gaze at Lex. "I thought you knew me better than that."

He did. "I don't think you were involved," Lex replied. Screw his friends, he knew her. Inside and out. "I saw your face at that station. You didn't know what was going down."

One of her delicate shoulders lifted in a move that was probably supposed to look careless. "Maybe I'm just a really good actress."

"Not that good."

Her chin notched.

Dev cleared his throat. "I *will* trace that money. I'll find out who was behind that hit."

"*If* it was even a hit," Sophie noted. "Maybe Griffin inherited money from a dead uncle. Maybe he sold furniture or a car. I'd call this circumstantial evidence, nothing more." Her voice dismissed them all. "Now, I have clients waiting at my office. This little stop was fun, but I'm done." She stared directly at Lex. "Done here. Thanks for your services, but they are no longer needed."

What?

She marched for the door, her heels sinking into the carpet.

He shook his head, pretty sure that she hadn't just told him he was fired.

But she was opening the door. *Leaving him.* "Sophie, dammit, wait!" He lunged forward.

Dev caught his arm. "Man, there is still more you don't know. More you probably don't want to know about her. She isn't what you think. Not at all. Save yourself some serious trouble and *let her go.*"

Maybe he liked trouble, because Lex shoved Dev out of his way and gave chase. So what if he looked desperate? She couldn't get away from him, not like this.

He caught her at the elevator. His fingers curled around her shoulder, and he swung her back to face him. "Sophie, no."

Her face was a perfect blank — no emotion at all. No fury. No pain. And he knew she had to be hurting. Hurting because if she hadn't been involved in the hit on Duvato — and, yeah, it sure sounded like a hit now — then she'd been used as bait for the killing. Maybe she'd been used by the one man she considered family.

"Get your hand off me," Sophie ordered. "I told you, we're done."

No, they weren't even close to being done.

He lifted her up against him and she gave a little yell. "What are you doing?" Sophie demanded. "Stop it! Put me down! *Now!*" Ah, that last word held plenty of emotion. Fire. Fury.

The receptionist came running. Her mouth dropped open as she stared at them in shock. Dev and Chance were right on her heels.

Sophie squirmed against him. He just tightened his hold.

"Uh, Lex…" Dev began. "I don't think you should—"

"Fuck off. You've done enough damage."

Sophie frowned down at him. She wasn't struggling in his arms. She was so warm and perfect. So Sophie. "Lex?" Her voice was softer now.

He carried her into his office and kicked the door shut. Then he let her slowly slide down his body. One sensual inch at a time.

"Wh-what are you doing?" Then she sucked in a sharp breath. "No, you don't get to manhandle me and carry me in here like some kind of—"

"I'm sorry," he told her softly. "I just wanted you to stay."

"Too bad." She jerked away from him. "I don't need your services any longer. But then, according to your buddies, I never did. I'm some scheming criminal mastermind who was just using you as a cover for my big plan of killing Daniel."

"You'd probably make an awesome criminal mastermind." He fully believed that.

Her brow furrowed. "Did you just insult me or compliment me?"

Lex paced to his desk. He opened the top drawer and pulled out her check. "You paid too much."

"Yes, well," she pushed back her hair, "let's just call it even and be done."

"I don't like that word. Done." He shook his head. "We aren't." Keeping his gaze on her, he ripped up the check.

"That's a ten-thousand-dollar check," Sophie said, lifting her right brow. "What was tearing it up supposed to prove?"

"That I don't give a shit about the money."

Her eyebrow dropped.

"That I plan to keep watching out for you, protecting you, until I've caught the man who broke into your place. The same man I'm damn sure tried to run us down in front of the courthouse."

She advanced toward him, then seemed to catch herself. "But what if I've just been scamming you? What if I'm just some cold-blooded killer and none of what I've told you before is true?"

"Then I'm a piss poor judge of character because I don't think you're cold-blooded." He tossed away the scraps of the check. "I don't think anything about you is cold." Lex headed toward her and pulled Sophie into his arms. "Not a damn thing."

***

He'd done it. Griffin Hollister tried to keep his face suitably stoic as he sat through the endless round of questions. He knew the drill, of course. He'd have to bide his time and play the role. The slightly shell shocked man who'd been forced to take a life.

As if a jerk like Daniel Duvato mattered in the grand scheme of things. The bastard deserved exactly what he'd gotten. Actually, he deserved more. For his crimes, the fellow should have suffered so much longer.

But his suffering hadn't been part of the deal. Duvato's death—oh, hell, yes. It had been.

And that twenty grand was just the start. Now that the job is over, I'll get the rest of my money. He just had to finish jumping through hoops first. He had to answer all the questions and play the scene just right.

Then, when the ADA let him go and all the police suits were out of his way, he'd collect his final payment and leave the country immediately. No one in DC would ever see him again. Because that, too, had been part of the plan.

Good-bye, asshole criminals. Hello, sun-kissed girls in bikinis. He couldn't wait to get down to the Caribbean.

CHAPTER EIGHT

Lex lifted Sophie up — she loved his strength — and pushed her back against the wall. Her legs curled around his hips, her skirt hiking up. She should be telling Lex to get his hands off her. She should be walking out that door.

But Sophie felt as if she were splintering apart on the inside, and he was the only anchor she had.

I don't think anything about you is cold.

She'd just wanted to run away from him. From Chance Valentine. From Chance and Dev's accusations. From the very real fear that, maybe, just maybe, Ethan had used her. That he'd set her up in one of his careful plans. That the one person she'd truly trusted in the last ten years had used her.

"Forget everything else," Lex rasped against her mouth. "Screw the others. Just focus on me. On you. *Come back to me, Sophie.*"

The small handbag she'd been carrying hit the floor. Her hands lifted and curled around him. Her nails sank into his shirt as she held him tightly. She wanted to be with him. Wanted to forget the rest of the world and just vanish with Lex.

Lex was heat. He was passion. He was need.

"I want you, sweetheart," he told her, the words a fierce growl, "so damn much."

She looked into his eyes and saw the truth of those words. His desire was plain to see. No lie, no deception. He stared at her with a fierce lust in his gaze, a desire darker and hotter than anything she'd seen before.

Had any man ever wanted her the way he did?

Had she ever wanted any other man this way?

No.

"Here," Sophie heard herself whisper. "Right now."

"Sophie…" Not an argument from him, but a hungry, wild answer. Then his right hand was pushing her skirt up even more. She still had on thigh highs, so she felt the rough touch of his fingers on her inner thigh. That touch electrified her and Sophie arched toward him because she needed the pleasure they could share.

It was the wrong place—his friends were just down the hallway.

It was the wrong time—she should be getting the hell out of there.

But if she didn't have him, right then, Sophie was afraid she'd lose her mind. She had too much pain ripping her apart on the inside. Too much fear and too many memories. She needed Lex and his passion to wipe everything else away.

"Fuck me now, Lex," she told him. "Now."

His fingers slid under the edge of her panties. She heard the rip of the material, and then his fingers were pushing into her sex.

"Sweetheart, you're so tight. I have to make you ready."

She kissed his neck. Bit him lightly and loved the growl he made. "I am ready. I want *you*." He had her pinned against that wall. His fingers were in her, but it wasn't enough. She wanted—

He stroked her clit. "You have to be ready. Always…ready."

Her breath choked out. Her thighs quivered around him.

"Not just…fucking…" Lex bit out. He kissed her. Deep. Almost angry. "Not with you."

Her heart seemed to stop. What had he meant by that? "Lex?"

"You are so perfect to me. Perfect *for* me." He kept stroking her, and she was wet now, her sex opening and slickening with his every touch. Sophie could feel her orgasm building. They were both fully dressed—well, okay, except for her ripped panties. Being with him like that, right there in his office, it made her feel even wilder. Turned her on even more.

They weren't in the dark. The lights were bright. She could see every expression on his face. So much desire filled his gaze.

"When you come, don't cry out," Lex said gruffly. "They're too close…"

His fingers slid into her — two big, callused fingers. Her own hands clamped down even harder on his shoulders. *In and out…stroking, stretching…*while his thumb pressed over her clit.

"You are the most beautiful woman I've ever seen," Lex said, "and when you come…"

She was about to come. She'd wanted his cock in her. Wanted him to fuck her hard, but he was bringing her to careful release, holding her tight, caressing her so intimately and —

His fingers thrust into her once more. Lex was working her sex faster now, a little harder, and still strumming her clit with his thumb as her breath heaved out. Tension tightened her body, driving up the need inside of her. Pushing her right to the edge —

He strummed her clit, and Sophie exploded.

"When you come, you're fucking gorgeous," Lex rasped. He kissed her again. Lex thrust his tongue deep even as his fingers kept stroking inside of her. She knew her sex was clamping tightly around him. She could feel the trembling contractions of her inner muscles. The pleasure came in rolling waves, knocking out her fear and her pain until he was all that she knew. Only Lex.

"*Lex.*" She'd whispered his name because his fingers were sliding out of her. Because he was carrying her now. Slowly sitting her on the edge of his desk. Then he lowered her skirt. And stepped back.

He hadn't come. "Lex?" Now his name was a question. She squeezed her thighs together because she was still quivering inside and she wanted that delicious quiver to last as long as possible.

"That was for you." But the desire was there, nearly burning out of control in his gaze. "Because I need you to know that I can be more than a selfish bastard. With you, I can be so much more."

Just like that, her heart was racing again. The tension between her and Lex shot up even more. His cheeks were stained red, his features harder, rougher with his need. A need he wasn't filling because…he only wanted her pleasure?

Sophie shook her head. "I want you."

"You need to want me more."

She didn't think that was possible.

"More than breath, Sophie. More than life. More than any man you've desired before—"

"I do." A stark confession.

"And more than any who will come again."

She didn't want to think of another lover. Only Lex.

"I need you to want me so much that the rest of the world can just fuck off because they don't matter. The lies and the games and the pain…none of it matters because you want me so much." His hands flew out and slapped down on the desk, caging her. "Because that's how I want you. I want you so much that I feel like I might just rip apart."

She wrapped her arms around his neck. Kissed his cheek. His mouth. Sophie lightly slid her tongue over his lips. "Then take me. I'm right here…"

"I won't be a bastard, not with you." She felt the shudder that shook him. "You matter."

Her heart hurt.

"Think about what you truly want, sweetheart. Because if you break your one night rule with me…"

Her lips parted. She had been about to break her rule! That stupid rule—the rule that never let a lover get too close. *He's already close.*

"I won't let you go. If I have you again, you're mine."

The look in his eyes…the intensity of his voice…Sophie swallowed over the lump in her throat. He meant exactly what he was saying.

"A man could get addicted to a woman like you. Hell, I think I already am. So caught up that

I'd be willing to do just about anything to have you again." Then he shoved away from the desk and from her. "But before I cross that line, you need to be sure. Be sure I'm the man you want, because there will be no going back."

Those words seemed like a dark warning.

Was she ready for that step? Was she ready for Lex?

"Then I'll know all of your secrets," Lex promised.

Instinctively, Sophie shook her head. No one knew them all.

"And you'll know mine. And I'll keep you safe, from anyone and everything that might try to harm you."

There seemed to be another layer in his words, a meaning that she wasn't getting. "I don't understand."

"Then let me be very clear. I don't care what you've done, Sophie. I don't care if you've had to attack in order to survive. I will protect you, and no one will ever take you from me."

I don't care if you've had to attack in order to survive.

She knew, then. The understanding pierced Sophie to her soul. He thought she'd killed her parents. And he was saying what—that he didn't care? That he'd still stand by her? No, not him. Not a protector like him, he wouldn't—

"I will protect you," Lex said again.

She jumped off the desk. "I have to go to my office." Her knees did a jiggle, but she didn't fall. Thankfully. "I have clients waiting. They need me." She ran for the door. Desperate, yes, she was a very desperate woman in that instant.

"I need you, Sophie."

His low words froze her as she was reaching for the doorknob.

"I think I need you more than I've ever needed anyone, but you need me, too, don't you?"

She looked back. "Yes." A faint whisper. She did need him. She needed him to banish her pain and her fear. Needed him to accept her just as she was.

And he is. He just said he doesn't care about my past. He just wants me. "Why?" Sophie asked.

"Don't you know? A smart woman like you, haven't you figured it out yet?"

She shook her head.

"You will."

Sophie shivered at the hot promise in his voice. Hurriedly, she bent and picked up the handbag she'd dropped in the, ah, heat of the moment.

"When you come to me again, sweetheart, I'll take you. You'll take me. And there will be no going back."

She opened the door. Hurried out. Made herself not look back. *Get to the elevator. Get to the elevator. Get —*

She was in the elevator. The doors were closing. She could breathe again.

A strong, tanned hand flew out, stopping those doors as the sensors immediately reacted. The doors slid back open. "Lex, no," Sophie began, "I told you, I'm going to my office —"

"And I'm making sure that you get there safely." Only it wasn't Lex standing there. It was Dev. His bright blue eyes met her gaze. "When I saw you run out, I figured it would be better if I came along, instead of Lex."

When he entered the elevator, she didn't back up. "Why?"

"Because Lex is too involved with you, he can't see you for what you are."

I think he may see me for exactly who I am. He was the only person in a very long time to do that. "No," Sophie said as the elevator descended. "I mean why does anyone need to come with me? I fired you guys." Talk about not taking a hint.

Dev laughed. "You are an interesting woman. Very dangerous, I have no doubt of that, but interesting."

Her head cocked. "If you think I'm so dangerous, then why get me 'safely' to my office? Surely I can handle myself."

The doors opened. They were on the street level. She'd just planned to snag a cab, only now it looked as if she'd be sharing that ride.

He kept perfect pace at her side. "I have no doubt that you can handle yourself, but I want to keep Lex fairly sane today. He and Chance will go find Griffin and get him to talk, and I'll make sure you're okay."

When had they come up with that plan? "I was with Lex, he didn't mention any of this—"

"Chance and I worked it out while you and Lex were, um, talking."

Was she supposed to blush? Stammer? Act embarrassed? She wasn't that girl. "He was giving me a great orgasm," Sophie said bluntly. "And thanks so much for asking."

His jaw sagged in shock. Perfect. Seizing that shocked opportunity, Sophie jumped into the cab that was waiting by the curb. "There's an extra twenty if you get me away from that jerk closing in," she rushed out to her driver.

The driver shot away from the curb just as Dev was reaching for the door.

Sophie tossed a grim smile back his way. *That's for calling me dangerous.* She had no doubt that he'd be tailing her in the next cab. Fair enough. She'd proven her point. *Don't piss me off.* Sophie yanked her phone out of her bag and immediately dialed Ethan.

He answered on the second ring. "Sophie, what's wrong?"

"We need to talk, but we have to do it alone." She leaned forward and gave the driver her firm's address. Then, settling back into her seat, Sophie whispered into the phone, "I don't like being used…"

***

"Sophie!" Sophie had just walked into her office when Kurt Blayne rushed toward her. But the guy didn't stop with an exuberant shout; he wrapped her up in a hug, holding her tightly. "I heard about what happened at the police station," Kurt said as he gave her a reassuring squeeze. "I'm so glad you're all right."

She held herself stiffly in his embrace. "I'm just fine." Since when was he into hugging her?

Kurt stiffened. He let her go, easing back. "Sorry, I was just worried." He exhaled and ran a hand through his normally perfect hair. Kurt knew that jurors liked perfect. "First, I heard about the near accident at the courthouse, and then the shooting this morning…it's just…" He exhaled roughly. "You gave me my break in this town. You took me on at the firm even though I had no fancy Ivy League diploma behind me."

Her brows rose. "I don't have one of those either."

"Yeah, but you're Sophie Fucking Sarantos. You make people notice you. You dominate in the courtroom. Getting to be second chair with you has been…" He straightened his shoulders. "A privilege."

Wow. Okay. Someone needed to cut way down on the caffeine.

"If something happened to you, they'd probably fire me," Kurt continued, his voice lowering. "You're the one who wants me here."

Ah, now that made more sense. She patted his shoulder. "You don't need to worry about your job. You're a great attorney. Trust me, the other partners here know that. If you weren't working with me, then one of them would just snatch you up." The guy would be going places.

"Really?" His shoulders straightened even more. And some of the worry eased from his face. "That's good to know."

If she hadn't been so damn stressed, she might've smiled. Self-interest could be such a powerful motivator. "Is Julianna here yet? I need to talk with her." Julianna Patrice McNall-Smith was the main client that Sophie needed to see that day. And seeing her, well, maybe it would take Sophie's mind off the craziness that was her current life.

I'll meet Ethan later. I'll figure this out.

"Um, she is here, but…"

But?

"There's a guy in waiting area one. He said it was urgent—that he had to talk only with you."

That news perked her up a bit more. "A new client?"

Kurt shook his head. "Not new. He said you'd handled his case before."

Her palms got a little sweaty. She felt *less* perky.

"His name is Finn Scott."

Sophie made herself smile. "I'll talk with Finn first. It won't take long. We just have a loose end or two that needs to be tied up." She pointed down the hallway. "Please make sure Julianna has some coffee and tell her that I'll be there soon."

Footsteps rushed behind her. She glanced over her shoulder, not really surprised to see Dev huffing and puffing as he rushed into her office. The receptionist, though, he looked plenty surprised when he saw Dev charging in on the scene, and Matt rose to his feet in alarm.

"It's all right, Matt," Sophie said quickly. "He's with me." For the moment. "Uh, Kurt, would you take Dev back for some coffee, in waiting room two? I'll deal with him in a moment." After she got Finn out of her office. One crisis at a time.

And if Dev saw Finn…

One at a time.

Dev tossed her a furious glare. "Don't ditch me again."

Seriously? Did he think she'd respond well to those words? "Don't piss me off again or I'll have Matt toss you out."

Matt immediately nodded. He was their receptionist and a part-time bodybuilder. If she said toss, he'd eagerly toss.

Now, for the first crisis. She turned to the left, heading toward waiting room one. Dev didn't follow her. Good news for the moment. And, even better, Finn was the only person in waiting room one. As soon as he saw her, he jumped to her feet. Sophie put her finger over her lips when he started to speak. "Let's go to my office."

Why was it that all of the secrets from her past seemed so determined to burst into her present?

***

"Are you a client of Sophie's?" The annoyingly GQ-looking fellow asked Dev. The guy led Dev through a winding hallway. "Because if so, let me assure you that Sophie will give you the best possible representation. She's the most talented lawyer I've ever met, and I consider it a privilege to work by her side."

Whoa. Someone was putting it on pretty thick. Barely controlling an eye roll, Dev brushed by the guy — he already knew the fellow's name was Kurt Blayne — because he'd done his research. He knew everyone in Sophie's life. He knew the woman far better than Lex did. *And that's the problem. Lex is lust blind. He needs to see Sophie for who she is.*

Kurt opened the door for him. "Just wait in here. I'll have fresh coffee brought in for you both."

Both?

Then he saw the woman. He recognized her instantly, mostly because Julianna Patrice McNall-Smith had been in the news so much recently. Her face had been splashed across every news show and put in every paper. When a woman that gorgeous was found in a blood-soaked room with her too rich husband's dead body a few feet away, well, that story was a reporter's wet dream.

Julianna glanced up when he entered the room. She gave him a quick, nervous smile.

The smile took him back. It didn't look like the smile of a femme fatale. And the fear in her eyes wasn't femme fatale material, either.

GQ must have thought so, too, because he inched closer to Julianna. "Got any special requests for your coffee?" His voice was low, gentle. "I can bring you anything you want."

Julianna's pale hands slid over the strap of her purse. "Nothing for me, Kurt, thanks. I'll just feel better when I see Sophie."

Right. Sophie was her attorney. If anyone could get the blonde off the hook for murder, it would be Sophie.

Even though the evidence against Julianna was supposed to be incredibly strong.

"She'll be right with you, Julianna," Kurt promised, and then he slipped from the room.

Silence. Julianna was on the couch. Her shoulders were hunched, her head down. She looked beaten.

He stepped toward her. She flinched.

What the hell? She hardly seemed like the spoiled beauty that the papers had made her out to be. Instead, she struck him as wounded.

A victim.

She was small, close to Sophie's build. Sleek and beautiful, no doubt, but…

Why do I feel like she's been hurt too much?

"You must be one of Sophie's clients, too," Julianna said, her voice breaking a little bit as if just speaking to him had been hard for her. "She's good. She makes you feel like you aren't the devil." Her shoulders hunched even more. "Even if the rest of the world swears you are."

Eyes narrowing, Dev took a step closer to her. She inched back against the couch cushions.

There was room to sit next to her, but he didn't. Instead, he took the chair to her right.

Her shoulders relaxed some.

Why are you so afraid?

"This is my first meeting with Sophie," he said, feeling his way along. But maybe Julianna could give him some intel he could use.

Or maybe I like talking to her.

"So I'm not sure what to expect," Dev added.

She glanced at him from the corner of her eye. She had deep, dark brown eyes, with flecks of gold near her pupils. "She'll make you feel like everything will be all right."

Is that what she did?

"You won't feel like a freak anymore when she's there. You'll feel like…" Julianna swallowed. "There's hope."

CHAPTER NINE

"Finn, what in the hell are you doing here?" Sophie asked as she shut her office door. "If you need to talk with me, just call."

"Your new lover came to my place, Soph. He came there…" Finn was pacing, fast, moving back and forth in a near blur. "And he accused me of trying to hurt you! He thinks I broke into your house, that I came at you with a knife!"

Tension gathered at the base of her neck. "He's investigating, nothing more. Looking at people who had access to my house."

Finn whirled toward her. In the rugged face of the man that he was now, she saw the boy he'd been. The boy she'd known so long ago.

"I gave him a list of all the men on my team. I know he's digging into their lives, trying to see if one of them did it, but I check those guys, Sophie! I always check. I would never hire someone…" Finn exhaled. "After what happened, I have to make sure my team is clean. If one of them did this and word gets out, I'll be ruined. Two strikes. My business won't come back."

"*If* one of those men did this, I'll handle it," Sophie assured him. "And I'll protect you." The way she'd done before.

Finn pressed his lips together. He seemed to hesitate, then he said, "If I find out one of them tried to hurt you…" His voice dropped. "I'll hurt him."

"No." She shook her head. "Absolutely not." Finn was a strong guy. And, when pushed too far, she knew he could be dangerous. Finn was an ex-boxer, a man with a lethal punch. Finn always tried so hard to control his temper, she knew that. *He's always been afraid of what he'd do if he was pushed too far.* She didn't want to be the person who made him cross that line. "I'm handling this situation."

He closed in on her. "But are you in danger? What can I do, Soph?"

What can I do, Soph? He'd said those same words to her when she'd been at her parents' funeral. Everyone else had been whispering and pointing at her. But Ethan had stood to her right, glaring at them all. And Finn had snuck up on her left. He'd taken her cold hand in his—her fingers had felt like ice that day—and he'd stood with her. Against the stares. The whispers. They'd grown closer after that. When she hadn't been able to stand the darkness any longer, he'd been her first lover.

But being with him hadn't changed the emptiness she felt.

"You don't have to do anything." She pushed back her hair. "I told Lex you weren't involved. He was just being thorough."

"Lex...the new lover." Finn gave a low whistle. "Be careful with him. The guy was possessive as all hell, acting as if he had some kind of claim on you."

If you break your one night rule with me, I won't let you go. If I have you again, you're mine.

"Doesn't he get that you're not in for some kind of forever haul?" Finn shook his head and the faint lines near his mouth deepened. "Or maybe you just weren't with me."

There was pain in his voice. She'd never meant to hurt him, but she had known that he cared, more than she did. "Finn, that was a long time ago. We were kids." She'd learned, after Finn, not to mix sex and emotions. She'd hooked up with men that she wouldn't be tempted to stay with past the night. Men she couldn't trust. Men she would never want to love.

Look what love did to my mother. She stayed with a bastard for years. She always professed her love, even when she just stood there and watched him hurt me. Her mother's voice rang in Sophie's head, "*I love him. I can't leave him, oh, no. You just have to be better. You have to be a good girl.*"

Maybe she hadn't wanted to be good.

"I loved you."

Oh, damn. "Finn…"

His smile was bittersweet. "You didn't love me. I knew that. But back then, I stayed by your side because I loved you. I'd been mooning over you for years, but you only seemed to notice me at your parents' funeral."

That had been because he'd faced the storm with her. "You stood by me," Sophie said.

There was a frantic knock at her door.

She didn't move. "You didn't have to stand at my side. You could have turned your back on me, too."

His smile was sad. "Of course I couldn't. I knew you hadn't killed them."

How? How did you know?

The knock came again. Even more demanding. "I'm sorry, excuse me for just a moment." She hurried toward the door. Sophie yanked it open. "I am with a client," she hissed.

"Yeah, I know," Dev threw back. "I want in on the little chat."

"Not happening." She drew herself up to her full height and really wished she had a few more inches. "And you are supposed to be in waiting room two. Why didn't Kurt keep you there?"

"He's out getting coffee." Dev stared her down. "And when I came looking for you, I happened to glance through your blinds…" He pointed to the blinds right near the door.

She should have closed those blinds.

"And I saw Finn Scott."

She heard Finn's footsteps heading closer.

"Such a coincidence to see you again, Finn," Dev said, raising his voice. "What happened? Could you just not stay away from her? I've heard she has that kind of effect on men."

"You have no idea what she does," Finn said, his voice cold. "And a man like you never will." His fingers curled around Sophie's shoulder. Squeezed. "I was there for you before, and I'll always be there for you. If you need me, come to me." Then he nodded toward Dev. "Get the fuck out of my way."

Dev lifted his brows, but stepped back.

Finn hurried away, his body tense.

"We cleared his workers," Dev said after a moment. "The four men on his team, the ones who had access to your house all alibied out. But guess what?"

She knew he was keeping his voice deliberately loud so Finn would catch his words. Sophie didn't bother to guess.

"Finn doesn't have an alibi. Turns out he was alone at his place, no lovers to see him. No neighbors who could confirm his alibi. So maybe your ex decided to catch up with you, in the middle of the night."

Finn kept walking.

She grabbed Dev and yanked him into her office. Then Sophie slammed the door shut and jabbed her index finger into his chest. "Make up your mind," she snapped at him. "Am I the victim—with some crazy stalker terrorizing me? Or am I a scammer? A criminal? Because you are about to drive me insane, and trust me, that is *not* a place you want me to be."

His brows shot up. His lips quirked.

She jabbed her finger a bit harder. "You really don't want to be on my bad side. I've put up with you so far. Dealt with your insulting accusations—"

"Why? Why did you put up with me?"

"Because you're Lex's friend." Her hand dropped. "And I figure if he bothers to be friends with you, then you can't possibly be the dick that you seem to be."

He laughed. The sound was warm. Not annoying. "Don't be too sure."

Her gaze raked over him. "How did you meet Lex?"

"I was in foster care with him," he said easily. "Me, Lex, and Chance…we all wound up in the same group home at the same time. We clicked."

She waited.

"Family isn't always blood."

She knew that. "Is that why you're going for my throat? Because you're worried I'm going to hurt your family? Don't you think Lex is a big boy who can protect himself?"

"I think Lex lights up like the fucking Fourth of July when he's with you."

She shook her head, an automatic denial.

"I've seen it." Dev's voice was flat. "He can't keep his eyes—or his hands—off you. He fell for you, and I'm worried about the lengths he'd go to in order to make you happy."

"I-I have another client to see." She smoothed her hands over her skirt. "If you want to play guard all day, fine, do it. But I have someone else who needs me."

He tilted his head to study her. "Finn Scott loved you."

Yes.

"You walked away from him. *That's* why he's on my suspect list. Provided, of course, that you and Ethan Barclay aren't just scamming us all."

She waited. Since he was blocking her way to the door, there wasn't much else she could do.

"But you have a habit of walking away on the men in your life. They try to get you back. Alec Farrell, Justin Allan, even Bruce Mitchum—they all tried, right? But you kept walking."

"If your digging online said they tried, then I guess they did." She was going to push him to the right and out of her path. Simple. Effective.

"I don't want Lex falling hard, then having you walk. There's one thing I can't tolerate in this world, and that's seeing my friends get hurt."

"You need to learn the difference between sex and love," Sophie said brutally. "Lex and I had a hookup, nothing more. You need to—"

"Huh. That's interesting." His gaze sharpened as he lowered his face closer to hers.

She shoved him back. Hard. "What's interesting?"

"When you lie, your eyes change. It's faint, but there, and your voice goes extra cold, like you're locking part of yourself down inside."

"I have a client," Sophie gritted out. "She needs me."

"Yes." He nodded, a small frown on his face. "I think she does." He moved a bit to the side.

Sophie strode past him.

"And I think Lex does, too." His voice was soft, so very soft, and she almost thought that she'd imagined those words.

***

He'd finally managed to answer all of the questions. Fucking finally. Griffin Hollister took his time walking out of the police station. He sure didn't want it to look like he was in any kind of a hurry. He had to play things cool and keep it all together for just a little while longer.

"Hollister!"

He glanced over his shoulder at that call. Two men were approaching him. Tough-looking SOBs. One had dark hair, one light. Both wore intent expressions.

He edged away from them. "I answered all the questions! I'm done for the day. My rep is inside—go talk to him!" Because those two walked with the tough, stalking stride of hunters, he figured they had to be cops.

But the blond shook his head. "I'm not interested in your rep." He was closing in fast. Griffin was at the edge of the sidewalk. Traffic buzzed near him on the street. "I want to know about you and about the twenty grand in your account."

No one should have found that, not yet. These guys were fast. He swallowed. "My uncle died."

"Bullshit," the dark-haired guy called.

His eyes raked them. "You're not cops." If they were, they'd already be dragging him back in the station.

"No, we're private."

Private? He grunted. "Then I don't have to talk to you." Actually, there was only one person he needed to see. The guy with his payoff. "I've had a really shitty day, and you need to back off." The blond looked familiar and he realized that guy had been there—right after he'd shot Daniel

Duvato. He'd been there, keeping close to Sophie Sarantos. "Why would Sophie send you after me?" Griffin asked, really confused now. "She should be glad the guy is dead."

He turned toward the street. He wasn't taking his car from the scene. He'd never be driving that ride again. He had instructions to follow. He was supposed to take a cab. Meet at an exact location for that sweet, final payment.

Gunfire exploded. The pain hit him immediately, white-hot, burning, right in the middle of his chest. He looked down and saw a bloom of red on his uniform.

"Shooter!" It was the dark-haired guy yelling — and he was yelling the damn obvious. Of course there was a shooter. The bastard had hit him.

But it was the blond who grabbed Griffin and yanked him behind a parked car even as another bullet blasted.

The blond snarled, "You see what's happening? You're a loose end to someone, and they're trying to eliminate you."

His chest felt like a damn gorilla was sitting on it. So heavy. Not burning anymore, just *heavy*. He tried to talk, but he was coughing. Did blood pour out of his mouth, too?

"Did someone hire you to kill Daniel Duvato?"

Yeah and the son of a bitch is now trying to kill me. He needed to suck in a breath, but couldn't. He'd just been hit once, right? Or had it been twice? Shit, was he making that wheezing sound?

"Did someone hire you?"

He managed to nod. "H-help…" The blond had to get him help. This couldn't happen. He couldn't be gunned down right in front of a police station.

Just like a hit wasn't supposed to happen *in* a police station. But it had.

"Who hired you?"

He could hear other voices. Help was coming. He didn't have to talk. If he talked, he'd just incriminate himself. He…

Why was he feeling so cold?

"Don't die with that secret on you."

Die? He didn't want to die. Griffin tried to say that, but more blood burst from his lips. And what was wrong with his chest? The pressure was gone, that heavy weight vanished. Now he just felt nothing.

Was his heart beating?

"Talk to me! Tell me who hired you!"

He didn't think it was beating.

He didn't think…

***

Cops swarmed the scene. When a shooting happened literally right in front of the police station, an army of cops should be expected.

The bastard has balls. To shoot Griffin Hollister, right there.

Balls. Or maybe he just had straight up insanity.

Griffin's blood was on Lex's hands. He'd put his hands over the gaping hole in Griffin's chest, and the man hadn't even seemed to realize that Lex was touching him. One look and Lex had known that Griffin wouldn't live long. He'd hoped to get the information he needed out of Griffin before the guy passed.

It hadn't happened.

"Clear the way!" EMTs rushed forward. Lex backed up more. He saw that cops were already searching the street. Chance stood to the side, talking to a captain and pointing to a building across the road. No doubt, Chance was showing the captain where he thought the shooter had been positioned.

He'd just been waiting to take his shot. Waiting for that perfect moment.

"What the hell?"

At the low snarl, Lex glanced over and saw the ADA. Clark stared down at the scene in shock. "What happened here?"

"Shooter," Lex said flatly, and like Chance, he pointed to the building across the street. "I guess the guy wanted to make absolutely sure Griffin couldn't turn on him."

"What?" Clark shook his head. "No, Griffin is—"

"He *was* a killer for hire. He was paid to take out Daniel Duvato." *But who paid him?*

Shock flashed on Clark's face. "He told you that?"

Lex swung away from the guy. He needed to see Sophie. With blood still on his hands and a dying man's image in his mind, he needed her.

But a hand grabbed him and swung him back around. Clark stared at him with shocked eyes. "He was really paid to kill Duvato?"

"And Griffin was shot before he could turn on the man who hired him." Lex smiled grimly. "But that bastard isn't getting away clean. I won't let him." There was no way he'd leave that guy out there, running loose, with Sophie possibly in his sights. "No fucking way," Lex promised. He made to move around the ADA.

"No," Clark said immediately. "You're a witness." He jerked his thumb over his shoulder. "Chance is a witness, too. You're both staying here until I can figure out exactly what the hell is going on here." He raked his hand through his hair. "Hired to kill? Right in front of me?" Clark blew out a rough breath. "What the hell is going on? Who is doing this shit?"

CHAPTER TEN

Julianna Patrice McNall-Smith was convinced she had a killer on her trail. Sophie did her best to reassure the other woman. When you were facing life in prison, panic was normal. So were some paranoid thoughts, especially when the prosecutor really was out to get you. But Julianna barely seemed to be hanging on by a thread, and no matter what Sophie told her, Julianna maintained that the real killer was after her.

Maybe she needs protection, too.

When Sophie finished her meeting with Julianna, she noticed that Dev seemed to take way too much interest in the other woman's exit. *Perhaps he can be the protection she needs.* Sophie filed that thought away for later.

Her immediate need was escape.

Sophie made sure Kurt was chatting up Dev when she slipped out the back exit. After all, she had another appointment to make, and Dev couldn't get in her way.

When she headed out the back door, a limo was already waiting for her. The vehicle idled by the curb and she slipped right inside. As she jumped in, Sophie thought she heard her name being called.

Maybe I didn't slip away from Dev as easily as I thought.

"Get us out of here," Ethan barked to his driver. "Now."

And they pulled away. She didn't glance back. She knew that shout had come from Dev, and she suspected he was either rushing to tail them or speed-dialing Lex.

Ethan raised the limo's privacy screen. "I didn't use you."

She sat back against the leather seat, trying to look relaxed. A very hard task. "A hit was put on Daniel Duvato."

He didn't look particularly surprised. His still fresh scars *did* make him look rather intimidating.

"Twenty grand was deposited in the bank account of Griffin Hollister."

He just watched her.

"You know who Griffin is. He's been a regular at Wicked lately."

"The guy likes to drink." Ethan shrugged. "Am I supposed to turn away paying customers? He knows his limits."

She wanted to cut through the BS. Sophie didn't know how much time she had before Dev caught them. Her running off with Ethan—yes, she knew it wouldn't look good. But she'd needed to talk with him, needed to look in his eyes, as she questioned him. "Griffin was paid to kill Daniel."

"So it would seem."

His cool voice was driving her crazy. Her hands clenched into fists. "Before Lex and his friends follow the money, why don't you do me the courtesy of telling me the truth?"

"I always tell *you* the truth." She easily heard that slight inflection and got that she was supposed to believe he lied to the rest of the world, but not her. Never her, right?

So she'd believed.

"I love you." There, she'd said it. "Just like a brother." And that was the way it was between them. "I know what you did for me, and I'll never tell a soul." Not even Lex. She'd take that secret to her grave. Even though, sometimes, that secret ripped her apart. *Did my mother have to die, too? Couldn't something else be done? And my father…*

Even though he'd hurt her, even though she'd wished he would just drop dead so many times, Sophie never would have done the deed herself.

Right?

She glanced down at her clenched hands. Maybe she would have eventually killed him. By the time her parents had been murdered, she'd already been toying with the idea of killing herself. She'd just wanted to escape the pain.

And Ethan had been just like her. She knew the truth. She'd seen his bruises over the years. His father had been just as twisted, just as fucking evil—no, more so—than her father. Only Ethan hadn't tried to run away. Ethan had fought back, once he was big enough. Strong enough.

Ethan killed his father.

And then he'd killed hers.

"Sophie, what the hell are you talking about?"

Her gaze shot up. Ethan leaned toward her and when he reached out to touch her clenched fist, she didn't flinch away. Mostly, she didn't.

"You know I'd give you every dime I had, so this isn't still about college, is it?" His eyes swept over her face. The driver kept going, but the privacy shield was in place, so Sophie knew he couldn't hear anything they said.

They'd never discussed this. Mostly because she hadn't been able to bear saying the words out loud. But the time for pretending was long gone. She knew exactly what Ethan was, at his core, and she'd still stood by him.

Did he use me? She didn't want to believe that. Sophie swallowed and said, "You killed my parents."

He sucked in a sharp breath and his hand flew up. Her flinch was instinctive that time because her father's hand had flown so many times.

But Ethan just lightly cradled her cheek. "Oh, Soph, you thought it was me?"

Her lips parted.

"I thought it was you." His eyes squeezed shut but his gentle touch remained on her cheek. "I got there and saw the blood. I knew what hell you'd been through, and, baby, I thought you'd done it. I left as fast as I could because I wanted to find you and help you."

Her stomach twisted. "I saw you running from the house. I-I'd just come back, and I saw you leaving."

Ethan's eyes opened. His golden stare blazed with emotion. "I would not have hurt your mother. I wouldn't have, Sophie. I hated that she didn't take you and leave, but I knew she was weak."

Be a good girl.

Sophie pushed that old whisper away.

"I wouldn't have left their bodies for you to find. I would have just made your father vanish." His hand fell away. "And to be honest, I was going to do that. I was building to it...after my father—" Ethan shook his head. "I was done. No more pain. Not for you and not for me."

"I-I didn't kill them." Her voice was too quiet. "It wasn't me." All of these years, she'd been covering for him. Telling the cops that she saw no one. Living with the accusations but...

All along, Ethan thought he was protecting me.

"Who killed them?" Sophie asked.

Ethan shook his head. "I wanted the evidence destroyed. *I thought it was you.*"

So that meant they'd both let the real killer slip right through their fingertips.

***

Lex glared at the one-way mirror on the wall to the right. The ADA had thrown his ass in an interrogation room. He knew Chance had been put into a similar room right down the hall. The fellow was treating them more like criminals than witnesses. They hadn't been the one shooting — they'd been trying to save Griffin! Not that they'd been able to do any good.

His phone rang, and he yanked it out of his pocket. When he saw Dev's number on the screen, Lex immediately took the call. "Tell me she's okay."

"She was...the last time I saw her," Dev muttered. "That was right before she slipped out the back of her office and jumped into a limo that I'm sure belongs to Ethan Barclay."

Son of a bitch.

"I would say this means she's been working with him all along." Dev's voice was grim. "That she's been using us to set up a perfect kill scene. But…"

"But?" He had the phone pressed tightly to his ear. His furious face stared back at him from that mirror. *Dev was supposed to stay close to Sophie.*

"But I think I was wrong about your girl."

"Sophie isn't a girl." *But she is mine.* "Why the change of heart? You were ready to condemn her earlier." That still pissed him off.

"Let's just say I know what she looks like when she lies now."

Hell, there they went. Dev had always thought he was some kind of human lie detector, that he could see all the faint tells that people had — those slips that gave them away. Lex generally thought that was complete bullshit. Dev had told him once that he spent so much time studying the intricacies of computers and codes that he'd learned to study people with the same intensity. That he could see their mistakes, their coding errors.

Bullshit.

"If I had to guess, I'd say Barclay is taking her to Wicked. He had his club fortified after Daniel's attack there, and if he wants a safe place to talk with Sophie —"

"I'm on my way," Lex said. He shoved the phone into his pocket and marched for the door. The knob turned beneath his hand and when he yanked open that door, Detective Faith Chestang was standing near the threshold.

Her brows climbed. "Going somewhere?"

"Yeah, to Sophie." The ADA was right down the hallway, just a few steps behind Faith. Lex glared at the guy. "Unless you're arresting me for something—and we both know you're not—then I'm out of here."

As if on cue, Chance opened the door to his interrogation room, too, and he stepped into the hallway, joining the little party.

"We're done here," Lex said flatly. "You need me for something else, come and find me." Because he needed to get to Sophie's side. Seeing her was his top priority. He could still smell Griffin's blood and could see the dying man choking on his own blood.

I need Sophie. Every instinct he possessed screamed that she was in danger.

Clark's jaw locked. His eyes glinted as he said, "Tell Sophie she doesn't have to worry about Ethan any longer." Clark's voice was rough. "Daniel never had the chance to talk. Maybe that was their plan all along."

What? Lex headed toward the ADA.

"I was going back into the holding room," now Clark spoke softly, the words carrying just to Lex. "Right before Griffin fired, I was going in there, but Sophie stopped me. She pulled me back and *that's* when Griffin fired. Why did she pull me back? I keep asking myself that question. And the only answer I get is that Sophie knew what Griffin was planning." He gave Lex a grim smile. "You're a blind fool, you know that? You think Sophie is interested in you, but she's always going to be tied up with Ethan. And that's where she is right now, isn't it? You're rushing off because you found out she was with him and you can't stand it."

There was just the faintest note of — jealousy? — in the guy's voice. So Lex just smiled at him, determined not to let the ADA see any of his emotions. "I know Sophie damn well. Ethan isn't a threat to me, and tonight, Sophie will *be* with me, not him. I'm not blind, and I know exactly where I stand with her."

"You don't know her…"

He didn't like people telling him that. "Trust me, I do. Far better than you ever will." Lex strode down the hallway, with Chance at his side. As soon as they cleared the building, Lex could see the uniforms still out sweeping and searching for clues across the street. Yellow police tape marked off the spot where Griffin's body had been, and blood stained the concrete.

"I'm going to Wicked," Lex said. "I'll take care of Sophie."

Chance nodded. "Dev and I will follow the money."

Because the money was their biggest lead. He turned to the right, but Chance caught his arm.

"Do me a favor, man?" Chance said.

Frowning, Lex glanced at him. Only he saw that Chance's gaze was on the building across the street.

"Don't get shot," Chance said flatly. "I don't like this case. Not one bit."

Who did? But Lex nodded and hurried away.

***

Wicked wasn't filled with dancers. There were no drunk men and women eager to escape into the wild beat of music at the club. The place was as silent as a tomb as Ethan led Sophie inside.

Dark. Too empty.

"All these years," Ethan muttered. He went straight to the bar and grabbed for the whiskey. "I thought I was protecting you."

"Who else would have wanted them dead?" She was the one with the biggest motive. When he poured two glasses of whiskey, she grabbed one and downed it in a quick gulp. "The rest of the world thought my dad was perfect—so big at church, great at his job. That's why none of the cops ever did anything. They bought into his lies." The monster had only come out at home.

Ethan drank his whiskey just as fast as she had, then immediately poured more. "So many years have passed. It's not going to be easy to track down the killer."

Maybe. Maybe not. She reached for her refilled glass, but didn't drink. "What if the killer has already tracked me down?"

He stilled, with that whiskey midway to his mouth.

"Did you send that man to break into my house?" Sophie had to ask that question.

Ethan slammed the drink down on the bar top. "Hell, no! I would never do that to you!"

She took a sip from the glass. She hadn't even noticed the burn of the whiskey during her first glass. She noticed with the sip. Weird. "The man who came in said he wanted to make sure that I was all right." Her mind wouldn't let this go. "He said he wanted to kill Daniel because of what he'd done to me."

Ethan's glass was still in front of him. He glanced around the bar, jaw tight, then he looked back at her. "And now Daniel's dead."

"Did you put the hit on him?" They could talk freely in Wicked. She knew that.

"No."

Was he lying? Would he really lie to her? Sophie stared at him, trying to see deep inside to Ethan's soul, wishing she could magically know the truth.

"I love you," Ethan told her. "You called me your brother, and Sophie, you have to know that I think of you as family. Every dark secret I have, you know."

He didn't know all of her secrets. He didn't know that she'd come close to taking her life right before her parents' death. *I wanted the pain to stop.* She'd been on that bridge, ready to jump, but she hadn't gone into the churning water.

Sophie took a longer sip — more of a gulp — and didn't feel the burn of the whiskey that time. "The man in my home wanted to kill Daniel because of what he'd done to me. Do you think it's possible…? No." She tightened her grip on the glass. "There's no way that same man could have killed my parents. That was so long ago. It wouldn't make any sense." Would it?

"No one has hurt you since then." Ethan's voice was considering. "No one but Daniel."

If she did have a stalker… it was almost as if the guy saw himself as her protector. Would Daniel's attack have set him off? After all of those years…?

Maybe.

"Ethan —"

A faint beeping filled the club's interior. Sophie stiffened.

Ethan didn't look concerned. "I put in a few security upgrades after the last mishap here."

Mishap? Is that what he was going to call the time he'd nearly died in that place, courtesy of Daniel?

"During the day, I have a security monitor in place that tells me when anyone gets a little too close." He tapped a button, and a screen appeared behind the bar. The shelves of glasses slid back, and the flat screen literally just appeared. Ethan tapped a button on his phone, and an image immediately appeared on that screen.

She saw the front exterior of Wicked.

She also saw a very determined Lex heading their way.

"Here comes the new lover," Ethan said. He glanced over at Sophie. "You sure you know what you're doing with that one? He doesn't seem like the type to let go easily."

No, he wasn't. He also wasn't the type to give up on someone. "I trust him."

Shock flashed on Ethan's face.

A bit self-consciously, Sophie tucked a strand of hair behind her ear. "And that's not the whiskey talking, okay? Lex is one of the good guys."

He tapped another button on his phone, and, on the screen behind the bar, she saw the door to Wicked swing open. *Remote controlled.* Handy.

"Since when…" Ethan asked, "do you date good guys?"

Lex quickened his steps and entered Wicked. "Since him," Sophie said.

Ethan swore, but she was already turning away from him. She hurried across the bar and met Lex seconds later. "Look, I can explain," Sophie began even as she wondered how he'd tracked her to Wicked. Dev, probably.

Lex caught her in his arms. He pulled her against his chest, holding her tightly. She could feel the frantic racing of his heart. Then—

He kissed her. Wildly, desperately.

"I am standing right here," Ethan called out. "And this shit is extremely awkward. It's like you're making out with my sister right in front of me. Stop it, seriously."

Lex pulled back, but only a little. He rested his forehead against hers.

"Lex, what's wrong?"

"Griffin is dead. He was shot right in front of me. There wasn't a damn thing I could do to save him."

She shook her head, an instinctive denial.

"The shooter was good. He hit from across the street. Sniper position. He took out his target then got the hell out of there before the police arrived." Lex looked over her shoulder, and she followed his gaze.

Ethan had the whiskey glass in his hand as he frowned at Lex. "Not me, man. I didn't hire anyone to kill Daniel. The guy was rotting in prison. He wasn't my concern."

"Bull. You came huffing and puffing to my house because you were afraid he'd turn on you. But he got shot before he could, then—bam— Griffin is taken out, too."

Ethan rolled his shoulders. "So you think that means I eliminated all of the ties to me. Clever, but—"

"Stop it!" Sophie nearly yelled. "Drop the tough guy act, Ethan! I told you, I trust Lex."

She felt the ripple of surprise roll through Lex.

"She's been drinking," Ethan said quickly. "Don't go getting all excited there, Lex. Whiskey makes her say crazy things."

The hell it did. She could drink him under the table any day of the week. "Drop it," she ordered Ethan again. "We need to find out who is doing this. What if he comes after me again? What then, Ethan?"

Ethan seemed to pale, but he nodded toward Lex and admitted, "I knew Sophie would stop the deal from going through, okay? I wasn't planning to kill the guy right there. And if—fucking worst case scenario—Daniel *had* talked, then I would have applied pressure directly on the ADA. It's not like that guy doesn't have skeletons in his closet. Hell, years ago, Clarke liked to go slumming on the wrong side of town. I saved his ass a time or ten, but he likes to act like that never happened."

She hadn't known that.

"And all the times that Griffin came here?" Lex wanted to know. "What was that about?"

"Man, I don't even stay here at night. Don't like the crowds." Ethan stroked the scar on his left cheek, then grazed the one on his right. "I'm not really in the mood for the ladies to look at me like I'm some kind of freak."

"You're not," Sophie said immediately.

Ethan laughed. "Soph, I've always told you, we have to do something about that soft heart." Then his face tightened as he focused on Lex once more. "I didn't even see Griffin so I sure didn't go hiring the guy to kill for me. Look somewhere else, and look fast."

Sophie opened her mouth, ready to tell Ethan that she'd fired the guys from VJS, so there would be no looking for them. That Lex was there because...

He wants me?

But Lex beat her to the punch. "Dev and Chance are already searching. We'll find the bastard."

"Good," Ethan retorted. "Because it almost sounds as if the SOB wants to make me look guilty. Been there, done that shit already, and I sure don't plan to do it again. I've got enough hell already on my plate."

Yes, he did.

"Let's go, Sophie," Lex said. His fingers twined with hers.

She nodded.

"Sophie!" Ethan's voice held a worried edge. "Be careful with him."

With Lex?

"Good guys can hurt you, too."

Lex pulled her closer to his side. "No, I won't. Count on that. I'd fucking take a bullet before I hurt her."

She could practically feel Ethan measuring Lex. Judging him. Finally, Ethan said, "Good. Remember that promise. I expect you to keep it." Then he waved them away. "Sophie knows the way out."

She did and she was the one who led them away from Ethan, and from the heavy darkness that always seemed to cling to him. A darkness that she'd known, too, for so long. But she was tired of the dark. Couldn't it be time for her to step into the light?

They didn't speak until they were at Lex's car. He opened the passenger door for her and she slid inside.

"I needed to see you." His voice was gruff.

Before she could reply, he'd hurried around the car and climbed into the driver's seat. She reached for his hand just as he was about to start the car. "I needed you, too." She needed him more than she'd realized.

He sucked in a breath and looked down at her hand. "Did you think about what I told you earlier?"

She glanced out of the front windshield. The sun was starting to set. In a few hours, when darkness really took over, Wicked would be packed. She didn't plan to be anywhere near the club then. She planned to be in bed with Lex. "How about we try for that second night?" Sophie forced a smile, hoping it hid her nerves. "Want to see if it will be as good as the first?" Her gaze slid back to him, and she saw his whole face harden, even as his eyes lit with a fire.

"I don't need to see."

His voice alone could turn her on—and did.

"I know making love to you again will be fucking fantastic." A muscle flexed in his jaw. "The hard part will be holding on until I get you home. When I'm near you, I want." It sounded as if he were just stating a fact.

It had never been that way for her. Having someone want her so completely. So totally. All of her flaws and secrets, exactly as she was.

A thrill shot through her and she leaned across the seat toward him. Sophie caught Lex's lower lip between her teeth, feeling reckless and wild with her own desire. She tugged sensually even as her hand slid down his chest. Down,

down to his waist, then to his crotch. He was turned on — she could feel the hot length of his cock through his jeans. "I want, too. So drive fast, Lex. Because this time, I'll get to make you crazy."

He growled and said. "Sweetheart, you already do."

She stroked him again, eased back in her seat, and smiled.

Lex spun the car out of the lot.

***

No, no, no! He sank back into the alley as fury pumped through him. This wasn't supposed to happen. Sophie wasn't supposed to turn to someone else. He was the one who'd done everything for her. He was the one who'd taken all of the risks. He'd *killed* for her.

But the bitch thought she could just go to another?

She was dead wrong.

No, no, Lex Jensen was the one who was dead. Tonight. Lex was dying tonight. And maybe he'd die in front of Sophie. Then she'd see. She'd realize all that he'd done for her over the years. She'd know that she belonged completely —

To me.

***

"Who the hell is that?" Ethan muttered beneath his breath as he stared at the security feed. He'd left the monitor up and he'd watched Lex play the gentleman and open Sophie's car door.

You'd better treat her like a fucking queen. She deserves that.

But, after they'd pulled away, Ethan had noticed something else. A shadow that shouldn't be there. Lurking, near the alley. A shadow that had the form of a man.

He unlocked his safe, took out his gun, and headed outside.

Ethan knew that shadow had been watching Sophie.

He searched the alley. The place reeked, but there was no one back there. *Not anymore.* Still clutching his weapon, Ethan returned to the front of Wicked.

Sophie was gone. Her watcher was gone.

This shit wasn't good.

CHAPTER ELEVEN

She wants to be with me.

Lex knew just how important these moments were for him, for Sophie, and he was determined not to screw anything up.

He shut the door at his house. Set the alarms. Looked around. The place wasn't good enough for her. He should light candles—do some kind of romantic gesture that women were supposed to like. Maybe he should get some wine for Sophie. Run her a bubble bath?

His gaze jerked around the room. The fireplace. Right. A crackling fire would be good. But first, he needed to get clean. He'd been surrounded by blood and death and before he touched Sophie, he wanted to wash that off his skin.

"Just relax here," he told her, his body actually aching because he wanted her so much. "I'll be right back."

She frowned a little bit, but he hurried down the hallway. He stripped and jumped in the shower, not caring that the water was ice cold.

Maybe it would slow him down a bit and help him to keep his control longer because when he touched Sophie, he pretty much went up in flames.

"I could join you."

He whirled around. The still cold water pelted him, and through the glass door, he saw Sophie standing there. Stripping.

Not fast like he'd done. But slowly, sensually. Her shirt. Her skirt. Her thigh highs. How many pairs of those sexy things did she own? As he watched, she unhooked her bra and smiled. Then she kicked out of her shoes and, with her gaze on him, she pushed her panties down her hips.

The water didn't feel so cold.

His hand flew out. He yanked off the faucet even as he opened that door.

Sophie waited a few steps away. She was completely nude. A perfect temptation. "I figure there is a reason you ran in here."

His gaze was on her breasts. Those perfect pink nipples. Sweeter than strawberries. "Couldn't touch you…" His voice was a rumble. "With death still on me."

He heard her surprised inhalation. Maybe he should have sugarcoated, but thinking was kind of hard then, what with her sex bare and so very close.

I want to taste her again.

He grabbed a towel. Yanked it over him. He was dragging that towel down his chest when Sophie touched him. Her fingers slid over his stomach, and he was the one sucking in a hard breath.

"Let me," Sophie said.

He'd let her do anything she wanted. Didn't she know that?

She took the towel and slid it down his chest. Every muscle locked down. Well, his cock shot *up*. He was hard and aching, and if his control didn't hold, he'd be coming all too soon.

She eased the towel down more. Put it right over his straining erection. Through the towel, she squeezed.

"Sophie, sweetheart, let me get you to the bed." Or wait, hadn't he been planning to light a fire? Or get wine or—

Planning to fuck her. Hard and deep. Planning to take her so completely there will never be another for her.

So much for good intentions. Every stroke had his primitive side—a side never too far away—surging forward.

Then Sophie dropped the towel. She leaned forward.

"Sophie—"

She put her mouth on him. A hot, wet heaven. She licked and she sucked and control disintegrated. He was supposed to seduce.

He barely stayed sane. His arms locked around her. He lifted her up, trying desperately not to hold her too tightly but—

"Are you going to fuck me?" Sophie asked. She arched up toward him. Bit his neck. He *loved* it when she did that. "Or do you want to make me wait while you shower again?"

The question shocked a laugh out of him and bought him a few more moments of not actually pouncing on her. He carried her to the bed. Spread her out. Looked his fill at her. "I was going to seduce you."

She smiled. A real, warm, actual smile. One that stole his breath and his heart.

"Didn't you notice?" Sophie murmured. "I just seduced you."

Hell, yes, she had.

He reached for the nightstand and Lex yanked on a condom that waited there. Sophie's eyes were on him, so watchful. "I can't be easy," Lex warned.

"Good. I don't want you to be."

"Hard. Wild?"

"Yes, please," she whispered.

Fuck, *yes.* He drove into her. As deep as he could. Her legs wrapped around him even as Lex yanked her closer. Her sex squeezed him and when he pulled back—*yes, yes!*—her core was a tight, wet clasp. He thrust into her, again and again.

He took her breast in his hand. Stroked the nipple. Applied just enough pressure to make her moan and arch up against him. His hips pistoned against her and then they were rolling across the bed. Sophie rose above him, her knees on either side of his hips. His hands clamped around her waist and he guided her, moving her faster. With her rising above him like that, she looked so incredibly perfect.

If possible, he felt his cock growing even harder for her. His right hand slid down, found her sweet spot, and stroked her. Sophie's hands slapped down on his chest as she moaned, but she kept rising and falling, rising and falling — then she was coming.

Her eyes met his, and Lex saw her gaze go blind with pleasure. Her hips slammed down against his once more as she shuddered. He drove his cock into her as deeply as he could, then he held himself still, gritting his teeth as he tightened his muscles. He could feel her sex squeezing around him with the contractions of her release. So good. Freaking amazing.

She choked out his name. Her nails scored his flesh.

Her sex contracted again.

Yes.

She slumped forward. He wasn't done. Not yet. He spun her so that she was beneath him in that bed. He lifted up her legs, putting them over his shoulders, and opening her even wider to him. Then he thrust. She was so warm and wet from her release, and he sank in to the hilt fast. The pleasure was so intense his whole body jerked.

"Lex!" His name was a sharp cry from her and he looked up immediately, afraid he'd hurt her. But pain wasn't on her face. Only pleasure.

Sweet hell, she's still coming for me.

He thrust into her. Claimed her. Got lost in her warmth and when his climax hit him, the release thundered through his whole body. His blood heated, his spine tightened, and he poured into her, riding a wave of pleasure so strong that his breath shuddered and his heart quaked.

When it was over, he slowly lowered her legs. He eased from her body and pressed a kiss to her lips. Lex ditched the condom then went back to her, carefully arranging the covers for her before he slid into bed beside Sophie. The lights were out. They were in the darkness. She was soft and sweet beside him.

In the dark, with pleasure still pulsing in his veins, he found that he could tell her his secrets. "I never had a normal life." His voice rumbled as he stroked her arm with his fingertips, enjoying the silk of her skin. "I was relieved when I entered foster care. Most folks think it's bad, but it was a million times better than the life I had at home. And there, I met my family. Chance and

Dev. We bonded, became brothers, and I knew I'd never be alone again." He kept stroking her. "Chance and I entered the military together, we fought together. We nearly died together." But he didn't want to think about those times. "Then we decided to look for a better life." When the fighting had been done. When his soul had felt too dark.

She pressed closer to him. Her hand rose and curled with his. "I never had a normal life."

He almost didn't breathe right then, because he knew — this moment — she was sharing her secrets with him, too.

"My father hurt me all the time. My mother watched, always telling me that if I was a good girl, if I just stopped being bad, he wouldn't have to punish me anymore. He'd stopped punishing her, after all, and he only turned his rage on me."

He lifted their twined fingers to his mouth and pressed a kiss to her knuckles.

"I knew it didn't matter how good I was. He wouldn't stop. So I started to think the only escape I had…was death."

Fear and fury whipped through him. Fear for what could have been. A world without Sophie. Fury because a young girl had been pushed so brutally far.

"But it wasn't my death that came. It was theirs. And for so long, I felt guilty because I wasn't sad. I didn't mourn them. I was happy." A brief moment of silence then, "I was happy because I was free."

"You didn't kill them."

"No, but I did lie to the police." Her voice thickened a bit, as if with a memory that hurt her. "When I got home, I saw Ethan running from my house. When I went in and found the blood, the bodies, I thought he'd killed them."

Lex still thought—

"But he was just protecting me. I learned tonight that he'd gotten to the scene before me. When he discovered the bodies, he thought I'd killed them. Ethan got rid of the weapon, to protect me."

Was that true? Or was Ethan lying to her?

"I don't know who killed them. For years, I thought I was protecting Ethan, but I wasn't. Someone else killed them, and I have no idea who it was."

I'll find out for you, Sophie. He pressed another kiss to her knuckles. "Why did you become a defense attorney?"

"Because sometimes, people do bad things, but only because they're pushed too far. They're pushed so far and so hard that they break. Some of my clients are broken, and they need my help to get pieced back together." She turned in his arms. "And some of them are just straight-up innocent. They need my help even more. I know what it's like to be looked at as if you were the monster in the room." Her hair slid over his arm as she shook her head. "I prove they aren't monsters."

He leaned down and kissed her. "You could never be a monster." He could, though. If something happened to Sophie, if he lost her now…

"We can all be monsters," she said, sounding thoughtful. "If we're pushed hard enough."

He opened his mouth to reply, but the ringing of his phone cut him off. Frowning, he glanced around the room.

"I think the phone is on the floor," Sophie said helpfully, "in the bathroom."

Hell. He climbed from the bed, thinking someone had just gotten on his shit list. He'd been in paradise with Sophie, actually getting her trust, then the call had wrecked the scene.

But it could be about her case. Get the damn phone, then get back to her.

He found the phone on the bathroom floor. He scooped it up and saw Dev's face on the screen. "What did you find out?" Lex demanded immediately. He made the mistake of glancing toward the mirror. His face was hard, tense, and stubble lined his jaw.

Sophie had seriously climbed into bed with *that*? He was such a lucky bastard.

"I've got a money trail," Dev said. "Didn't take too long. A couple of false leads but…guess who paid Griffin twenty grand?"

"Cut the crap and tell me," Lex snapped. "I'm ready to kick the guy's ass." Because it was all connected. Every single bit—

"Finn Scott."

"What?"

"It took some tracking, but I found a separate account that the guy had, one from a bank in Grand Cayman. Tricky bastard. It looks like he's been funneling money down there for years. But I caught him. He's the one who paid Griffin."

And he was Sophie's lover. A man who might not have been able to let go of her.

"Do you know where Finn Scott is right now?" Lex wanted to know.

"Chance and I are on the way to his house. We should be there in about ten minutes."

He needed to be there, too. If that jerk really was the one who'd done all of this…*has he been obsessed with Sophie for all these years?* "Finn knew her before her parents died," Lex said, his mind spinning. "Hell, it's possible he's even the one who killed them." Finn would have known about Sophie's pain. Maybe he'd wanted to end that pain and punish those who'd hurt her.

The same way he'd wanted to punish Daniel?

"Give me the address," Lex said. He had to confront Finn himself. This was Sophie's life they were talking about. Lex needed to be there. Right damn then.

Dev rattled off the address.

"Good. I'm on my way. And, hey, watch your ass, okay? If this guy is the one who took out Daniel today, he might be waiting at his house, armed." And ready to take out anyone who came close.

"You just keep Sophie safe," Dev replied. "Chance and I can handle this SOB."

Lex lowered the phone. His rough reflection still stared back at him from the mirror, but now that reflection wasn't alone. Sophie was there, wrapped in a white sheet. Her hair tumbled over her shoulders. Her eyes — so big and deep — met his in that mirror. She looked delicate, sexy.

His.

"Who is it?" Her voice was incredibly calm. "You know now, don't you?"

He nodded. "Finn."

Her reflection showed her pain. Lex turned toward her, wrapping his arms around Sophie's shoulders. "Dev traced the twenty grand back to him, back to an account that Finn had in Grand Cayman."

"He still had that account?"

She knew about it?

"He set it up years ago, when he was afraid he'd be convicted. I told him it was a terrible idea, but he was panicked. Finn was so afraid he'd lose everything he'd built. I warned him that if the district attorney's office found out, Finn would just look even more guilty." She bit her lower lip then said, "He told me he got rid of that account."

"Yeah, well, he lied." *And probably killed.* "He's not the man you thought." Lex gave her a reassuring squeeze before he hurried from the bathroom. He grabbed some clothes from his closet and dressed as fast as he could.

"You're going after him."

"Chance and Dev are heading to the guy's place now. I plan to provide them with backup." He heard rustling behind him. He looked back and saw that Sophie had taken clothes out of her bag. She was dressing even faster than he was, sliding on jeans, a sweatshirt, boots. "Sophie..."

"Don't even think of telling me to stay here, Lex. This is my life. I'm confronting him. I get to find out why he did this to me."

Lex wanted her to stay locked in his house. He wanted her safe. Always, but...

He also understood her. Sophie wasn't the type to hide from the pain around her. She was a fighter, and she was right—this was her life.

He headed toward her. Lex kissed her. Hard, deep, fast. "You stay behind me." Because the memory of a flying bullet and the spray of blood was too fresh in his mind. "If he's armed, you don't even think of disobeying my orders. I won't have you put at risk. You matter too much."

Her lips curled into the faintest of smiles. *I will never grow tired of her smiles.* "Because I'm awesome in bed?" She seemed to tease him.

He wasn't teasing. "That's not why."

She blinked and even looked a little insulted.

"You're fucking amazing in bed, but that's not why," he clarified quickly. They should be clear on this. "You matter because I love you. I love every damn thing about you."

She shook her head. "We…no, don't say that."

That was hardly the response he'd hoped to get, but Lex said again, 'I love you."

Her eyes filled with tears. "You don't. It's too soon. Don't say it and don't make me think I matter like that to you. Don't make me think you want me—"

"I want you forever." He should be racing out of the house. Going after Finn. He wasn't moving. "I want you at my side for the rest of my life. This isn't some sudden thing for me. I started falling for you weeks ago. When I first met a tough, smart lawyer in a police station, and, for just a moment, she made me forget my own name."

She swiped her hand over her cheek. "You thought I was a potential suspect back then, you thought—"

"I thought I wanted you, no matter what. I thought you were sexy as hell and the desire I felt for you was fierce, but the more I learned about you, the harder I fell."

"Lex…"

"I'm not asking how you feel about me." They'd get to that, later. He'd try to be better. Charming. He'd try to be whatever she needed. "I just thought you should know. For me, this isn't just another case. It never was. It was always about protecting you." His fingers grazed down her cheek. "Loving you."

Her breath whispered out.

"Now let's go find the son of a bitch who paid for that hit," he said. Time to end the nightmare for her. Because when the nightmare was over, they could plan for a future—he could start courting her. *Courting her.* Yeah, it sounded corny as hell, but he wanted to do things right with Sophie.

A normal life. Maybe they could both have that—together. They hurried through the house and were outside in moments. They'd almost reached his car when the flash of headlights illuminated his driveway.

Sophie lifted her hand, shielding her eyes. Lex stepped in front of her. A visitor? Now? He didn't have time for this crap. He opened Sophie's door. "Go ahead," he told her, "I'll get rid of whoever this is."

Sophie slipped inside. He slammed her door. His visitor had braked and was climbing out of the car. The headlights were still on, and the driver had positioned the vehicle in such a way that those lights still blasted right onto Lex. It was a bigger vehicle. Lex figured it for an SUV.

Like the one that nearly ran us down outside of the courthouse. His body tensed.

"Lex!"

His head cocked at the shout.

"Lex, it's Clark Eastbridge!" A shadowy form moved from the car. "I have to talk with you."

The guy wanted to talk now?

"I have more questions to ask you about the shooting today." Clark was closing in.

"Your questions have to wait." He turned his back on the guy and hurried toward the driver's side of his car. "Or maybe you should come with us to see Finn Scott—"

It was the reflection that warned him. The reflection that showed Clark racing forward and lifting his hand.

Fuck!

Lex dove to the left even as gunfire blasted. He hadn't moved fast enough, though, and that bullet drove into his back, hitting him near his left shoulder blade.

"I'm done waiting," Clark said.

He fired again.

The bullet hit Lex and he fell forward. His head slammed into the rough cement of his driveway.

CHAPTER TWELVE

"Be careful," Dev warned Chance as they closed in on Finn's home. "If he's our sniper, then he could have us locked in his sights right now."

"Hardly the shit I want to hear," Chance said as he advanced.

"It's the shit that could save your ass," Dev replied, his voice no more than a whisper.

They were near the front door now. Chance glanced at Dev, then he rammed his fist against the door. "Finn Scott! Open the door *now!*"

They heard a crash from inside. The thud of footsteps.

"Running," Dev said, but Chance was already moving. Lunging away from the front door and heading toward the side of the house. Dev followed right after him. Just because Dev wasn't some ex-military hotshot like Chance, it didn't mean he couldn't handle himself. *Any day. Any night.*

He and Chance burst around to the back of the house. Moonlight shone down on them, and he saw Finn's fleeing form. Finn had something in his hand, and the guy threw it back.

Dev swore, but nothing exploded on him. Whatever that object had been, it had just crashed into the ground.

Chance crashed into Finn. He tackled the other man, and they rolled across the ground.

Dev stood over them, his breath appearing as a little cloud in the chilled air. He *could* have taken down Finn, but if Chance wanted to play action hero, why argue?

When Finn tried to swing at him, Chance drove his fist into the guy's jaw. Finn fell back, but then he growled like an animal, surging up—

Chance raised his fist again. "Don't even think it. You aren't armed now, and I can kick your ass in an instant."

Finn glared at him. "What do you want?"

Dev cleared his throat. Finn's head jerked toward him. "*We* want to toss your ass in jail," Dev said. "We know you arranged for Daniel's death, and we're thinking that once the cops search your house, they'll find the gun you used to kill Griffin Hollister."

"What?"

Chance stood and jerked Finn to his feet. "It's over. Dev traced your money trail. We know about the account in Grand Cayman."

"I don't even know what the hell is happening." Finn sounded furious. "I saw you guys sneaking toward my house. I figured you were coming to attack me!"

Dev rolled his eyes. "Chance and I are working for Sophie." Okay, maybe she'd fired them. Technically, they were freelancers on this one. "You know Sophie. She's the woman I'm pretty sure you're obsessed with. Did you break into her house? Just had to get close, didn't you? What happened?" Dev pushed. "Did Duvato's attack drive you over the edge? You realized that you'd nearly lost Sophie, so you had to act? Had to touch her, had to—"

"You are insane," Finn said grimly. He tried to wrench out of Chance's grip. Chance didn't let him go anyplace.

"I'm not the one who paid Griffin twenty grand," Dev said. "That would be you. Say goodbye to freedom, and hello to being someone's bitch in jail."

"I don't know any Griffin! And I don't have that account in Grand Cayman anymore!" Finn snarled. "Sophie told me to ditch it, and I did! Years ago! That's not me! I didn't pay anyone—"

Chance shook him. Hard. "Are you obsessed with Sophie Sarantos?"

Finn stopped talking.

"Can't let her go, can you?" Chance's voice was full of disgust. "You hurt her when you broke into her place. Lex told me she fell down the stairs. What if she'd died then? What if—"

"I didn't break into her place! Yes, dammit, I still have a thing for her, but I know it's not going anyplace. Sophie never loved me. I don't think she can love anyone, unless it's Ethan and that twisted-ass relationship they have."

Dev hesitated because the guy sounded…truthful?

"I gave up getting her back years ago. She's my friend, that's it. I would never hurt her!" Finn's breath heaved out. "As for Daniel…"

Sirens screamed in the night. Swearing, Dev looked over his shoulder.

"Cops?" Chance muttered. He dragged Finn toward the front of the house. Sure enough, the swirl of blue lights was coming closer.

Dev remembered when Finn had thrown that object at them. *A phone.* "You called the police."

"Hell, yes, I did!" Finn sounded gleeful now. "When two jerks come sneaking toward my house in the dark, what else is a normal person supposed to do?"

It *was* what a normal, *innocent* person would do.

The cop cars screeched to a stop.

But if Finn was innocent…

Then who was stalking Sophie?

"Everyone, calm the hell down!" A woman's voice rang out—Detective Faith Chestang. He recognized her I'll-Take-No-Shit tone. She approached with her weapon drawn. "I'm in command here!" She tossed a glare toward Chance. "As soon as I heard the call come over the scanner, I connected the dots. With everything going down with Sophie and her background with Finn Scott—yes, I know all about that, I'm a damn detective after all—I suspected I'd find you out here."

Her gun wasn't aimed at Chance or at Dev. She was pointing straight at Finn.

And he'd sure been ready to bet that Finn was guilty too, but now…what if they were looking at the wrong man? What if someone else had just wanted them to think Finn was guilty?

Finn was another longtime part of Sophie's life. A friend, a confidant. By making him look guilty, that man would be removed from Sophie's world, perhaps tossed permanently in jail.

And the ADA already said he wouldn't rest until Ethan was locked up.

Ethan, the other constant in Sophie's life. "I think we need to find Ethan Barclay," Dev announced. A gut instinct.

"Hell," Faith said. "That guy always means trouble." Her breath expelled on a long sigh. "This case is just getting worse."

Yes, it was.

***

Gunfire. Sophie had ducked as soon as she heard that thunder, and now she crouched in Lex's car, her heart racing. She didn't hear anything outside. She didn't hear Lex at all.

Not Lex. He can't be hit. Not Lex.

Her fingers fumbled as she looked for a weapon. She shoved her hand under the passenger seat and she felt the rounded edge of a handle. She pulled that handle, yanking it hard, and Sophie saw that she'd grabbed a screw driver. *Yes!*

Her car door opened. The vehicle's interior light flashed on and she looked up, hoping desperately for—"Lex?"

It wasn't Lex.

ADA Clark Eastbridge stood there. He smiled at her. "It's okay. You're safe now."

No, she wasn't. "Where's Lex?"

Clark offered her his hand. "Someone was waiting in the dark. They shot at him, and he gave chase. But it's okay. I'll take care of you until he gets back."

She stared at his offered hand. She'd tucked the screwdriver up the sleeve of her sweatshirt, instinctively hiding it when the car door opened. She didn't see a gun in either of Clark's hands. But maybe he'd hidden his weapon, too. How hard would it have been to tuck a gun in the back of his pants? Or to hide it under his jacket? "Why are you here?"

"Sophie." Now anger pulsed in his voice. "We need to get out of here. I told Lex I'd watch out for you. Come on." Then he stopped waiting for her to take his hand. He locked his fingers around her left wrist and pulled her out of the car. She didn't fight him, not then. What would have been the point? She had to wait for a perfect moment.

He kept his hold on her and headed back toward his vehicle. "I had a few more questions about the shooting Lex witnessed today." He was speaking quickly and guiding her to his SUV — a vehicle that still appeared to be running. Its bright lights were on. Why the brights? "I was here to talk with him, but the shooter must have come to eliminate him — and maybe you, too. Lex raced after him…"

He'd said that before. He spoke in that easy, confident voice that he used in the courtrooms. So sincere. So charming.

But she was scared and cold and she didn't see Lex. "Clark…" Her voice didn't tremble. That was good. "Did you ever get a hit on the traffic camera that was outside of the courthouse? Did you get the video of the vehicle that nearly ran Lex and me down?"

A vehicle that sure had looked a lot like this one.

"No." His sigh was long. Almost sad. "I'm sorry, Sophie, but it turned out there was some kind of glitch that day. No video was recorded."

Right.

He opened the SUV passenger door for her. Because she hadn't fought him, because she'd been so docile—maybe that was why he let her hand go. As soon as he did, though, she seized that moment and raced back toward Lex's car—toward the *driver's* side of his car.

"Sophie, *no!*" Clark called out. "The shooter—"

Lex was lying facedown on the ground. He didn't seem to be moving at all. She immediately dropped to her knees beside him. "Lex!" She touched his back and her fingers were instantly soaked in his blood. "Lex, no!"

Footsteps thundered toward her. "You should've just gotten in my vehicle."

Her head whipped back toward him.

Clark towered over her. "But maybe it's better this way. Now you can see that he's gone."

Lex wasn't gone. Her left hand was on his back, in his blood, but she could feel him breathing. He was still alive. Could Clark not see that small movement in the dark? The bright lights didn't hit over here. Maybe he didn't know…

You screwed up. Lex is still alive. And I won't let you kill him.

"He wasn't right for you, Sophie. He didn't believe in you. Never understood you."

Lex understood her perfectly.

"I've waited so long for you." Clark's fingers brushed over the back of her head in a caress that sent her stomach rolling with revulsion. "I first saw you years ago. Beautiful Sophie with the haunted eyes. I knew the first time I saw you that you would be mine."

She would never be.

Sophie kept her head bent. She began pulling the screwdriver from her sleeve.

"You were walking with Ethan Barclay. You'd been crying. I could see the tears on your cheeks, and I wanted to take your pain away."

She had no idea what he was talking about.

"So I started learning about you. Everything I could. Watching you. I loved to watch you. Did you know that sometimes, I'd even sneak into your house? It was so easy to get inside. That way, I could be close to you."

She felt Lex's muscles tense beneath her hand. When he'd been shot, had he fallen against the car? Or hit his head when he collided with the ground? She knew he'd been unconscious moments before, but that growing tenseness told her that he was becoming very aware again. She could feel him, almost as if he were readying for an attack.

Lex can't attack now. He's hurt! And Clark still had the gun.

"I watched you as often as I could back then. I even saw you that night on the bridge. You were climbing up there, and I was afraid you'd jump."

OhmyGod.

"I knew then just how much you needed me. I was there to take your pain away."

She shook her head.

But he kept talking. Clark said, "Since I knew my way in your house, it was easy enough to get in the night I killed your parents."

The world stopped spinning. He'd just said the words so casually. So calmly.

"Evil people should be stopped." He sounded as if he were speaking to a jury. Convincing them of just how just he was. "They should be punished. That's what I do, Sophie. I'm a prosecutor. I punish the criminals. Even way back then, I knew what I was meant to be. My first year of law school…" His voice actually *warmed.* "I killed them on a school break. No one ever had any clue."

The screwdriver was in her hand.

"I got nervous. I'll admit that." His hand stilled on her hair. "I left the gun. Stupid mistake. A mistake that could have cost me everything. But you covered for me, didn't you, Sophie? I rushed back to the scene, determined to get rid of all the evidence I'd left. I mean, hell, it *was* my first kill. I got nervous. I just didn't expect all of that blood."

No, based on the emotion in his voice, he'd gotten *excited*. Not nervous.

"But I saw you when I went back."

Because, apparently, he'd made a habit of getting in and out of my home – for how long? Dear God, for how long? Had she ever been safe from him?

"You threw the gun into the river for me. I followed you that night. You went back to that same bridge. You were so beautiful. I knew that you appreciated what I'd done for you. You felt the connection, too."

I feel that you're insane.

Her muscles bunched as she prepared to lunge at him and attack. She had to move fast, before Lex launched at the guy.

"You're such a dumbass, ADA Eastbridge…"

Those low, growling words came from right behind Clark. And that rough voice – she knew that voice. It was Ethan's voice.

Ethan was striding forward from the darkness.

"She didn't hide the gun for you. She did that for me. Sophie thought she was protecting *me*. Why the hell would she do it for you? She had no fucking clue who you were."

Clark's hand fell away from her, and, snarling, he whirled to face Ethan. As he did,

Sophie saw him yank a gun out from under his jacket.

"No!" Sophie cried.

"You're just some obsessed asshole—" Ethan shouted.

Sophie knew Clark was going to shoot him. She lunged to her feet and she drove her screwdriver into Clark's back as hard as she could. He bellowed and whirled as grabbed for her. She heard his gun explode and a white-hot pain lanced over her arm.

The bastard had shot her.

"*Sophie!*" That roar was Ethan's.

Clark yanked her closer against him. He put his gun under her chin.

"You attacked me." He seemed confused. *Why* would he be confused? Didn't he get that he was the bad guy?

She didn't like bad guys, not anymore.

She ignored the burn in her arm.

"Sophie, I'm so disappointed," Clark murmured. "After all I did for you! I mean, I even put Daniel in the ground. *For you.* I made sure Griffin couldn't talk—"

"You killed him," she whispered.

He nodded. "And then I ran to the scene, joining in the hunt for…me."

Such a twisted bastard.

"I'm a really fantastic shot," Clark said, raising his voice. "But even a piss poor shooter would still kill this close."

"Let her go!" Ethan yelled.

Clark shoved the tip of the gun deeper into the underside of her chin. He tugged her around a bit, moving so that they both faced Ethan. "You have your weapon, Ethan. Instead of pointing it at me, point it at yourself. Lift it up, and put it right to your temple."

Insane. She clawed at his hand, but he didn't so much as flinch. Was her screwdriver still in his back?

Ethan wasn't moving. She could see his still form.

"Put the gun to your head or I will shoot her right now!" Clark yelled.

That yell had her flinching.

And it had Ethan lifting the gun. "No," Sophie whispered. What the hell was he doing? She couldn't see his gaze, not in the dark. It looked as if he were staring right at her. He couldn't do this. Couldn't!

"You love Sophie, don't you, Ethan?" Clark never moved his weapon.

Ethan didn't speak.

"Let's see how much. Either you pull your trigger or I will pull mine."

No!

"Pull your trigger…" Clark shouted. "Or I pull mine!"

"No!" Sophie yelled. "No, don't you do it, Ethan! He's not going to kill me!" She was supposed to buy that this crazy freak had been secretly stalking her for years and *now* he was going to kill her in a blink? Bullshit, bullshit, bullshit. He was just trying to play some kind of head game with Ethan.

No, he's trying to get rid of Ethan. He's trying to get rid of everyone in his way. Lex, Ethan…

Ethan had his gun pointed at his temple.

"If you do it," Sophie shouted, "I will kick your ass!" She fully believed Clark wouldn't kill her—okay, she thought he wouldn't kill her right *then*. So that meant she could fight him. If he had the chance, though, hell, yes, she thought Clark would kill Ethan—and he'd finish Lex. *I won't give him the chance.*

"I knew you were trouble, Clark," Ethan said. He didn't sound frightened. He sounded pissed. "The first time your rich ass came into my neighborhood. You wanted drugs, and I told you I didn't run that shit. But you saw something else that got you addicted, didn't you? You saw *Sophie.*"

"Sophie was meant to be mine! She never loved another man, barely let any other lovers get close. She held herself back, for me!"

Ah, and now she knew just how to break free. "Newsflash, there, ADA Eastbridge. Lex got close."

His hold slackened.

"Want to know just how close?" She made her voice go velvety, husky. Seductive. "So close that *I love him.*" Sophie drove her elbow back into his stomach and when he grunted, she lurched forward.

"*Run, Sophie!*" Ethan bellowed.

No way. She wasn't going to run and leave Lex. She needed a weapon, she needed—

"And I…love…her…" Lex snarled.

Lex.

She looked back. In the dark, he'd risen. He grabbed Clark and threw him against the side of the car. The screwdriver hit the ground with a clatter. She lunged for it, but when she looked up, Clark was trying to aim his gun right at Lex.

"*Stop it!*" Sophie screamed. "Don't you hurt him! Don't!" She would stab that bastard right in the heart.

She didn't have to.

Lex knocked the gun out of Clark's grasp. She knew he broke Clark's wrist because she heard the crunch of bones. Then Lex pounded his fist into Clark's face again and again. Clark attempted to fight back, but he was no match for Lex's fury. No match for him at all.

Sophie stepped forward, but hard arms wrapped around her. "Let him finish the bastard," Ethan whispered in her ear. "Then you'll never have to fear Clark again."

Lex was in a killing fury. His wounds didn't seem to slow him down at all. His hands struck in a blinding rush, and the thud of flesh on flesh—the crunching of bones—had her shuddering. Lex wasn't stopping.

And she couldn't watch him murder a man. "He isn't you," she told Ethan.

His arms fell away. Sophie hurried to Lex. She reached out, touching his shoulder. "No more."

At her touch, Lex stilled instantly.

Clark slid down the side of the car, then fell, slamming face first into the cement.

Lex turned. He stared down at her. His eyes glittered.

"I'm okay," she told him. "He's done."

Lex's hand—bloody—reached out to touch her. But right before his fingers slid against her skin, his hand clenched into a fist. "I...love you." His voice was so rough.

"I love you, too." Saying the words wasn't hard. In fact, it just might have been the easiest thing she'd ever done in her life. She threw her body against his, holding on tightly to Lex. "I love you."

His arms closed around her.

Clark. Clark did this. The ADA! She couldn't wrap her mind around that, couldn't understand it all, not yet. In that moment, it didn't even matter. Lex was alive. She was alive — *that* was all that mattered.

Sirens wailed — seemingly far off.

"Someone called the cavalry." Ethan's voice was mild. "That usually happens when shots are fired. Tell you what…how about I kill this asshole before the boys in blue come rushing to the scene? Trust me, this ending will be better for everyone. Lex can still be your hero, you can sleep peacefully at night, and I'll feel one hell of a lot better about the world in general."

She shook her head, but didn't let Lex go.

Killing like that…there had been enough death. She didn't want it. "He killed my parents. He killed Griffin."

"There's not going to be any evidence to tie the guy to those crimes," Ethan argued. "He's slick. Hell, he'll just toss out some insanity defense and get away with it all. So what if he actually *is* insane? He's been hooked on you for years. You think he's ever just going to let you walk away from him?"

She couldn't *kill.*

Lex seemed to stumble against her. Her hold tightened on him. "Help me, Ethan! Clark shot him." She'd thought he was all right. The way he'd fought, but…

Lex was sagging. Slumping.

Ethan hurried forward. "Shit. When you've got bullets in you…" He slid his shoulder under Lex's right arm. Sophie put her body under Lex's left arm to help brace him up. "Maybe let me do the ass kicking?"

Lex grunted. "You were…busy…about to shoot…self…"

"I saw you moving behind him. I knew you just needed me to keep him distracted." They were shuffling forward. Moving toward the flash of blue lights. "I did my part, buddy. You're welcome."

Sophie glanced back. The men weren't even looking at Clark. Was he still breathing?

"Now do yours…"

Wait, had Ethan just said those words? They'd been so low she thought she'd imagined them. They shuffled forward more. The cop cars raced toward them. The first vehicle braked with a screech that hurt Sophie's ears. The driver's side door opened and —

"What happened?" Faith Chestang shouted. "Seriously…*let me handle this shit sometime! Don't always fight on your own!*"

Then she was running forward.

And there was a rustle behind Sophie. The whisper of clothing?

"Mine…" Such a low, furious growl. "Or…no one's…"

Clark wasn't dead, and, apparently, he still had a whole lot of twisted rage left in him.

Lex shoved Sophie to the side. Ethan shouted her name and the guy *jumped* on her. *What?*

And—

Clark ran toward them. He had the screw driver in his hand. The screwdriver that had fallen when Lex was fighting him. Clark had that screwdriver raised and was charging forward.

But he didn't get very far. Because Lex fired at him. Just shot with cold precision. Once, twice. The bullets sank into Clark's chest, hitting perfectly in the heart.

"No one owns Sophie," Lex said. His arm lowered when Clark hit the ground.

Ethan rose, moving off Sophie. "And now it's over."

"*Damn, damn...*" Faith ran forward. She kicked the screwdriver away from Clark's still form. "The ADA just went batshit."

No, he'd been batshit for a very long time. He'd just been good at hiding his dark side. Sophie was on the ground, the cement biting into her hands. Lex walked toward her, his steps slow, but not staggering. Had he really been that weak before? When he'd suddenly needed both her and Ethan at his side?

The gun was Ethan's. Lex took it from him. When Ethan had gone to Lex's side, that was when Ethan must have slipped him the gun.

She shook her head.

I did my part, buddy. Ethan had said that. *Now do yours.*

Lex stared at her. "I love you."

More cop cars rushed up to the scene. An ambulance was there. And—Dev? Chance Valentine? Yes, they were running toward Lex, too.

But Sophie hadn't moved from the ground. Lex had just killed in front of her. She knew—with utter certainty—that Lex had known Clark would attack again. He'd waited. He'd planned that moment perfectly.

Clark had attacked right in front of a cop. Faith had seen everything. She would testify—like it would ever come to that—that Lex had fired in self-defense.

But Clark hadn't been attacking Lex again. He'd been coming for me.

"He always would have come for you," Ethan said softly as he leaned forward and offered her his hand. "Don't you see that?"

She saw that Lex had killed for her. She'd never wanted that. She hadn't wanted him to ever carry that darkness for her.

Dev and Chance were surrounding him now. Talking fast. An EMT was trying to reach out to Lex.

He was just staring at her.

Her lips felt numb as she called, "He's been shot. Please, get him in the ambulance! Lex needs help."

But Lex shook his head. "I just…need you."

No, the man needed stitches. Maybe a blood transfusion. Definitely medical assistance.

"Only you," Lex said.

"I didn't want this," she whispered.

Pain flashed on his face. Even in the darkness, she could see it—those too-bright flashing police lights had let her see it. Then Lex was turning from her. Letting Chance and Dev and the EMT lead him to the ambulance, and she knew that he'd misunderstood her.

Dammit.

"Sophie, you know what he did for you," Ethan murmured.

The police were swarming the scene.

Her legs felt locked in place. "I never wanted him to do it. I never wanted anyone to kill for me." Because *that* was her greatest fear. That someone would be pushed to the edge—for her. She kept her voice whisper soft as she said, "For years, I thought you'd killed for me. Do you know how that cut me up on the inside?" It had terrified her and made her determined not to let anyone else get close. Because she'd been afraid that she twisted people. That she took the good and put a monster in its place.

But Lex isn't a monster.

He was in the back of the ambulance.

"What did I do," Sophie asked, "that fucked Clark up so much?" She didn't even remember meeting him so long ago. Had she?

"You didn't do a damn thing. That guy always had problems. I knew it the first moment I saw him."

Drugs. He'd gone to Ethan for drugs.

"Some men think everything should belong to them—everything and everyone. It's about control and power. That freak was high on his power. Being ADA, he got to control life and death for everyone around him. And you—oh, Soph, I think he wanted to control you most of all."

No one owns Sophie. Lex had said that.

When she looked back to the right, the ambulance was pulling away.

CHAPTER THIRTEEN

"Staying in the hospital for a bit longer probably wouldn't have been the worst idea in the world," Dev murmured as he sauntered into Lex's office with his brows raised. "But if you wanted to play superhero and act like bullets bounce off your chest, fine by me." He didn't bother closing the door behind him.

Lex was sitting in his desk. Very *carefully* sitting at his desk because he had plenty of stitches in his back. "They didn't bounce off my chest," he said flatly. "They hit my back. Actually, my shoulder and my left side." The bullets and blood loss hadn't been nearly as bad as the concussion he'd gotten when his head had hit that pavement. He'd lost consciousness for a few moments and woken up to absolute terror.

Sophie, in danger. Sophie, touching him…and talking to a demented bastard.

"Thanks so much for clarifying," Dev said with an eye roll. "Point is, you should be resting. If not in a hospital, then at least at home."

No way. When he was alone, he thought too much—about Sophie. About how he'd totally fucked things up with her because...*I killed a man right in front of her.*

But Clark had been running toward her. He'd had that screwdriver up and—

Why even try to kid myself? I took that gun from Ethan because I didn't think Clark was done, and I had wanted to be ready. If he'd come at Sophie again, I planned to kill him.

And I did.

Now he needed to find a way to fix this mess. He needed Sophie.

"So what are you going to do?" Dev wanted to know. "I heard Detective Chestang cleared you so everything is all tied up, nice and neat. The ADA was the psychotic bad guy. He was the one who took over Finn's account. Tricky bit of business, that."

Yes, it had been. Clark had found out about Finn's account when he prosecuted the guy years before, and he'd taken it over, secretly. Clark had been funneling his own money into that account over the years.

Clark had wanted Finn to appear responsible for Griffin's murder. Probably just a way to eliminate another man from Sophie's life. Daniel's attack on her had definitely set Clark off—severing whatever ties to reality that had held the guy in place.

Or maybe, as Faith had said, Clark really had just always been batshit. Who the hell knew what he'd been doing in his spare time over the years? Maybe there were more skeletons—and murders—still hidden in his closet.

"I heard some folks at the prosecutor's office are even thinking Ethan Barclay isn't the devil in disguise any longer. Clark was the one always pushing for a prosecution against him. Now that everyone knows the truth about Clark..." Dev shrugged. "Well, all of his cases are tainted. They'll have to be reviewed. Talk about a serious nightmare for someone."

Lex rubbed his aching temples. Since it seemed Dev had just gotten the inside scoop from the prosecutor's office, he wanted to ask, so badly, about—

"When are you going to see Sophie again?" Dev said, voice casual.

Lex's hands flattened on the desk in front of him. "You were at the scene. You heard what she said." Words that had hurt far worse than the bullets.

"Yeah, she said, and I quote, 'I didn't want this.' *This,* man. *This,* not you." Dev huffed out a breath. The door was still open behind him. "She was looking at a blood bath. Seeing the dead body of the guy who'd offed her parents. The woman should've been entitled to say anything she wanted right then, and you should have just been grateful she was still alive."

Lex surged to his feet and ignored the pain that burned through him. "I am grateful," Lex snapped back. "Do you know how fucking scared I was when I woke up and I could hear Clark talking to her? He was trying to take her away from me. I didn't have a weapon, and he had a gun. I had to get the gun away from him, I knew it. But I couldn't have her hurt." His words were coming faster, harder. Lex couldn't stop now. "She matters to me. More than anything. So, fuck, yes, when I got her away from that bastard, I hit him. I just kept hitting him." Through the blood and the crunch of bones. "I hit him even when he wasn't fighting back. I hit him because I *wanted* to kill him. I wanted her to be safe."

Lex's breath heaved out. *Slow down.* Apparently, he wasn't as in control as he'd thought.

"But you stopped…" Dev put his hand up behind him—what was up with that? It looked like he was almost waving to someone out in the hallway. "You stopped then," Dev said.

"I stopped for Sophie. She touched me, and I just wanted to hold her." But he'd been scared to touch her with blood on his hands.

"Then why did you kill Clark later?"

Growling, he shot around the desk. "Why the inquisition? Why—"

"Because you're sitting in here, and you're throwing something really important away instead of running out and making Sophie listen to you. So maybe…" He backed out, retreating from the room as he continued, "Maybe I'm trying to make you fight."

Lex blinked. Seriously? The guy had just walked out in the middle of the conversation? Dev could be weird sometimes.

But then Dev was back. Only he wasn't alone. He was pulling Sophie with him. Her eyes were bright with tears.

Had she been outside that door, the whole time? Listening to him rant?

And bare his soul?

Lex stiffened.

"Why did you kill him?" Dev asked once more.

Sophie shook her head. "Stop. Just stop, okay?" It sounded as if she were begging.

Sophie should never have to beg.

Her sigh was broken. "It doesn't matter why. What matters is that I pushed him that far." She wasn't looking at Dev. Instead, she was staring straight at Lex. "And I'm sorry. I never wanted that for you. I never wanted you to kill for—"

He had her in his arms. He had to touch her. Had to kiss her. Had to lift her up against him, and so what if he popped a stitch? Sophie was there. She was hugging him back. She was kissing him back. She was *there,* with him.

"I'll just leave you two alone," Dev said. The door clicked shut.

Lex didn't let Sophie go. He couldn't. "I'm sorry," he said. "Sorry you had to see me like that." With her, he would confess all. "I tried to pretend I was someone else with you. But that's *me*, sweetheart. When your life was threatened, I reacted." Primitive. Deadly. "I wanted you to love me, but…"

"Oh, Lex, I do love you." Her body pressed to his. "I told you that, and I meant it. I love you so much that it scares me."

He was the one scared — of losing her.

Sophie's beautiful gaze searched him. "I don't want you to ever be hurt because of me. I don't want to push you to the edge."

I'd go over any edge for you.

Sadness slid over her face. "Dev told you once that I was the wrong kind of woman. And he's right. I can be —"

"He's full of shit, and he knows it."

She blinked up at him.

"Didn't you notice just how much Team Sophie he is right now? He knows I love you. He knows I would do anything for you." Lex's voice roughened. "He knows that I was falling apart without you in my life."

"My life wasn't the same, not without you." Her hand lifted and slid over the stubble on his jaw. "I couldn't stay away any longer."

"And I was already making plans to seduce you back to my side."

"You were?"

"I was going to start with flowers." That had been the first plan. "Champagne. Maybe get one of those little bands to come to your office and serenade you."

Her lips lifted, just a little. An *almost* smile.

"I was going to do *anything* to win you back. To prove to you that we were worth fighting for." Lex swallowed as he tried to find the right words. This moment mattered so much, and he didn't want to screw it up.

But she nodded. "We are worth fighting for. You're worth fighting for." She squared her shoulders. Sophie looked so heartbreakingly gorgeous and determined as she said, "I want to be with you."

"Hell, yes." His instant response.

"I want to spend all my nights with you."

"*Always.*" Excellent plan.

"I want to wake up next to you."

Damn straight. No other man would be getting close to her.

"I want you to love me…"

"So much it hurts," he promised her.

Alarm flashed in her gaze.

"But in that very good way," Lex was quick to reassure her.

There it was — she smiled at him. A flash of her white teeth that made warmth in his chest. Her eyes lit up. She freaking lit him up.

"And I want you to know…" Sophie said, "that I love you, completely, totally, and I will love you for the rest of my life."

He lifted her up, holding her tighter, and whirled toward the desk.

"Lex, no, your stitches!"

He sat her on the edge of his desk. "Fuck them," he said.

She smiled up at him. He would *never* tire of her smile. "I'd rather fuck you."

That could totally be arranged. He kissed her again. But not hard. Not wild. Soft. Sensual. And as he kissed her, Lex knew…*I'll be asking her to marry me soon.*

But he'd do that part right. With flowers. With champagne. And with that band that he'd already paid to go and sing at her office. They were scheduled to arrive in the morning. Maybe that proposal would take place then, too.

After all, why wait? When you found something this good — this precious — a smart man held on tight.

Her arms curled around him.

Tight.

"I fucking love you," Lex said right before his lips pressed to hers.

EPILOGUE

Devlin Shade knew it was way past time to leave the office. Chance had checked out hours ago, and Lex — well, that guy had rushed away a few moments ago with Sophie. They'd been kissing, laughing, and kissing some more.

They'd been happy.

He was whistling as he waited for the elevator. Maybe he'd go and catch a basketball game. Maybe he'd —

The elevator doors opened. A damn drop-dead gorgeous blonde appeared. Not just any blonde.

Julianna Patrice McNall-Smith.

Her breath caught when she saw him. "You."

He'd been thinking the same thing. *You. You're the one I want. You shouldn't be here. You should be very, very far away from me.*

Because his body had a far too primitive reaction to her.

The elevator doors started to slide closed. He threw up his hand, stopping them.

She tensed and fear flashed in her eyes.

"Easy," Dev said. "Look, I think you got the wrong impression of me before. I'm not —"

"A killer?" Julianna laughed, and the sound was brittle. "No, that would be me, right? At least, that's what the world thinks." Then she shook her head, "I know you're not one of Sophie's clients. She told me earlier today that you worked here at VJS. I just wasn't expecting to see you, not as soon as I arrived." She leaned forward and peered over his shoulder. "Is there someone else —"

"There's me," he said flatly. "What can I do for you?' She'd made him curious. A dangerous thing.

She walked out of the elevator. Her hands twisted in front of her. He could practically feel the nerves rolling off her.

"Julianna," he prompted and — for some weird reason — he liked the way it felt when he said her name. "What can I do?"

Her long lashes lifted. "You can keep me alive."

His eyes widened.

"I'm really not the killer, you see. Someone else is, and he's after me. The cops think I'm lying. They won't help me, but you...you can." Her voice broke just a bit. "Please. I'll pay any price. I just — I don't want to die."

And she wouldn't be dying, not on his watch.

###

Available in February, 2015
Need Me (Devlin and Julianna's Book)

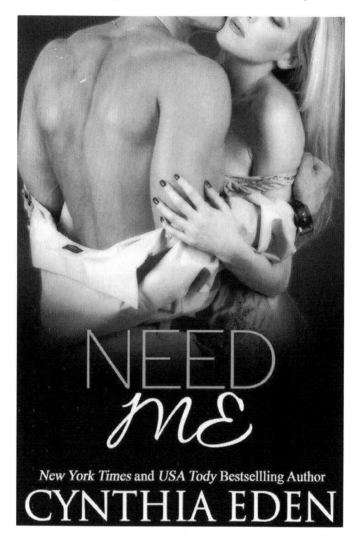

NEED
me

New York Times and USA Tody Bestsellling Author
CYNTHIA EDEN

And available now…

WATCH ME (Dark Obsession, Book 1):

Watch Me... The first book in New York Times and USA Today best-selling author Cynthia Eden's sexy new romantic suspense series…*DARK OBSESSION.*

He was hired to protect her.

Watching gorgeous Gwen Hawthorne wasn't a hard job—but it certainly was tempting. Chance Valentine had tried to keep his distance from the sexy socialite for years, but when her father hired him to keep watch on her—as a twenty-four, seven bodyguard—Chance knew his control was about to be pushed to the limit.

He'd never wanted another woman the way he desired her. Hot. Intense. Consuming. Being so close to Gwen, Chance knew that he wouldn't be able to resist her. So he gave into his need, *her* need, and he took them both to the edge of a dark and consuming desire.

But Chance soon realizes that he isn't the only one watching Gwen. Someone else is out there, a stalker who won't rest until Gwen is destroyed. Every day, every moment…Gwen is in danger.

And Chance knows that if he can't unmask the stalker, then he may just lose the only woman he has ever loved.

A NOTE FROM THE AUTHOR

I really appreciate you reading WANT ME. Thanks for taking the time to check out my romantic suspense novel.

If you'd like to stay updated on my releases and sales, please join my newsletter list www.cynthiaeden.com/newsletter/. You can also check out my Facebook page www.facebook.com/cynthiaedenfanpage. I love to post giveaways over at Facebook!

Again, thank you for reading WANT ME.

Best,

Cynthia Eden

www.cynthiaeden.com

ABOUT THE AUTHOR

Award-winning author Cynthia Eden writes dark tales of paranormal romance and romantic suspense. She is a *New York Times, USA Today, Digital Book World,* and *IndieReader* best-seller. Cynthia is also a two-time finalist for the RITA® award (she was a finalist both in the romantic suspense category and in the paranormal romance category). Since she began writing full-time in 2005, Cynthia has written over fifty novels and novellas.

Cynthia is a southern girl who loves horror movies, chocolate, and happy endings. More information about Cynthia and her books may be found at: http://www.cynthiaeden.com or on her Facebook page at: http://www.facebook.com/cynthiaedenfanpage. Cynthia is also on Twitter at http://www.twitter.com/cynthiaeden.

HER WORKS

List of Cynthia Eden's romantic suspense titles:

- MINE TO TAKE (Mine, Book 1)
- MINE TO KEEP (Mine, Book 2)
- MINE TO HOLD (Mine, Book 3)
- MINE TO CRAVE (Mine, Book 4)
- MINE TO HAVE (Mine, Book 5)
- FIRST TASTE OF DARKNESS
- SINFUL SECRETS
- DIE FOR ME (For Me, Book 1)
- FEAR FOR ME (For Me, Book 2)
- SCREAM FOR ME (For Me, Book 3)
- DEADLY FEAR (Deadly, Book 1)
- DEADLY HEAT (Deadly, Book 2)
- DEADLY LIES (Deadly, Book 3)
- ALPHA ONE (Shadow Agents, Book 1)
- GUARDIAN RANGER (Shadow Agents, Book 2)
- SHARPSHOOTER (Shadow Agents, Book 3)
- GLITTER AND GUNFIRE (Shadow Agents, Book 4)

- UNDERCOVER CAPTOR (Shadow Agents, Book 5)
- THE GIRL NEXT DOOR (Shadow Agents, Book 6)
- EVIDENCE OF PASSION (Shadow Agents, Book 7)
- WAY OF THE SHADOWS (Shadow Agents, Book 8)

Paranormal romances by Cynthia Eden:
- BOUND BY BLOOD (Bound, Book 1)
- BOUND IN DARKNESS (Bound, Book 2)
- BOUND IN SIN (Bound, Book 3)
- BOUND BY THE NIGHT (Bound, Book 4)
- *FOREVER BOUND - An anthology containing: BOUND BY BLOOD, BOUND IN DARKNESS, BOUND IN SIN, AND BOUND BY THE NIGHT
- BOUND IN DEATH (Bound, Book 5)
- THE WOLF WITHIN (Purgatory, Book 1)
- MARKED BY THE VAMPIRE (Purgatory, Book 2)
- CHARMING THE BEAST (Purgatory, Book 3) - Available October 2014

Other paranormal romances by Cynthia Eden:
- A VAMPIRE'S CHRISTMAS CAROL
- BLEED FOR ME
- BURN FOR ME (Phoenix Fire, Book 1)

- ONCE BITTEN, TWICE BURNED (Phoenix Fire, Book 2)
- PLAYING WITH FIRE (Phoenix Fire, Book 3)
- ANGEL OF DARKNESS (Fallen, Book 1)
- ANGEL BETRAYED (Fallen, Book 2)
- ANGEL IN CHAINS (Fallen, Book 3)
- AVENGING ANGEL (Fallen, Book 4)
- IMMORTAL DANGER
- NEVER CRY WOLF
- A BIT OF BITE (Free Read!!)
- ETERNAL HUNTER (Night Watch, Book 1)
- I'LL BE SLAYING YOU (Night Watch, Book 2)
- ETERNAL FLAME (Night Watch, Book 3)
- HOTTER AFTER MIDNIGHT (Midnight, Book 1)
- MIDNIGHT SINS (Midnight, Book 2)
- MIDNIGHT'S MASTER (Midnight, Book 3)
- WHEN HE WAS BAD (anthology)
- EVERLASTING BAD BOYS (anthology)
- BELONG TO THE NIGHT (anthology)

Made in the USA
Lexington, KY
05 April 2017